Robert Ken...

VANITY DIES HARD

RUTH RENDELL

BALLANTINE BOOKS • NEW YORK

Copyright © 1966 by Ruth Rendell

Originally published in Great Britain under the title
In Sickness and in Death.

ISBN 0-345-34952-0

This edition published by arrangement with Doubleday & Company, Inc.

Printed in Canada

First Ballantine Books Edition: December 1970

23 22 21 20 19 18 17 16 15 14

For the Savilles:
Patricia and Derek,
Mark and Caroline

Vanity dies hard; in some obstinate cases it outlives the man.

ROBERT LOUIS STEVENSON: *Prince Otto*

1

THE RAIN STOPPED AS THEY CAME INTO THE TOWN, but puddles lay everywhere, whipped and wrinkled by the wind. Wet leaves smacked against the windscreen and lay on the pavement like torn rags.

'This do you all right?' Hugo asked. He pulled the car on to a parking area marked with criss-crossed white lines as if for some intricate game. 'We're a bit tight for time, so if you think you can...'

'You might take her all the way,' said his wife. 'I call it mean, dumping people as if you were a bus. Besides, it's going to pour.'

'I said we were late,' Hugo snapped. He turned to his sister, 'O.K., Alice? Now the programme is, Jackie and I make a quick tour round Amalgamated Lacquers—there's some kind of a reception at four—but we should be through before five. Pick you up here again at five?'

'Lovely,' said Alice. She gathered up her umbrella and her handbag and opened the car door.

'Don't take any notice of him,' Jackie said quickly. 'Of course we'll call for you at Nesta's. Tell me the address again, will you?'

'Saulsby—S,a,u,l,s,b,y—Chelmsford Road, but I can easily—'

'Rubbish.' She glared at her husband and her black saucer-sized curls vibrated like antennae. 'If he had an ounce of—of chivalry...Oh, what's the use?' For Hugo had already started the car, was putting it in gear. In silent rage he held his left wrist extended, displaying the face of his watch. Alice stood on the pavement and gave a little wave.

'Love to Nesta and all that,' Jackie shouted. 'I hope she won't be in one of her moods. Mind you cheer her up before we come.'

In one of her moods....It was not improbable; it would account for her long silence, her apparent refusal to answer most of Alice's letters. Perhaps she shouldn't have come. Certainly it would have been better to come in her own car, instead of impulsively begging a lift from her brother. Chelmsford Road might be anywhere, might be a mile away on the other side of the town.

So this was Orphingham, a narrow high street rather consciously unspoilt, houses that were called 'period' because they had mostly been built before the nineteenth century, a few new shops, plane trees from whose trunks the bark peeled like flakes of olive-coloured paint. Above her on a bright green mound Alice could see the castle; between gaps in the buildings the Orph could be seen winding between water-meadows. Alice thought it had changed little since the days when Constable painted it, a brown looped river walled with willows. A pretty place for a woman of taste, or a sanctuary for a weary spirit.

Outside the town hall there was a street plan, framed and glazed. Alice found Chelmsford Road at once. She smiled at her own trepidation when she realised that Nesta's street was one of the arms leading from the junction where she now was. As soon as she entered it she saw that it was literally what it called itself, the road to Chelmsford. Wider than the street by which she had entered, it was affluent rather than beautiful and suggestive at first of a wealthy suburb. Many of the houses lay back, half concealed by high walls with gates let into them under arched openings.

It was not quite what she had pictured for Nesta. She had imagined a cottage with espalier apple trees and a porch of cockle-shells. 'A little house,' in Herrick's words, 'whose humble roof is weatherproof.' There was nothing like that here, only huge gabled and turreted villas. Nesta probably had a flat in one of them.

A light drizzle had begun to fall. Alice put on her grey uncompromising 'Pakamac' and opened her umbrella. As she did so she couldn't help remembering how perfect Nesta always looked, how svelte. Her umbrella had been a pagoda-shaped affair, black with a slender handle that looked as if it was made of onyx. Alice sighed. Even without a mirror she knew exactly what she must look like, a pleasant, blue-eyed English-woman, no longer very young and never worth a second glance. She put up her left hand to smooth back a trailing strand of fair hair and as she did so a raindrop splashed her new wedding ring. The sigh changed to a smile. What did anything matter, age, indifferent looks, competition, when she had Andrew?

She began to walk briskly down Chelmsford Road. As she had supposed from Nesta's address, none of the houses had numbers. Orphingham Lodge—the abode surely of a successful dentist—El Kantara, The Elms.... On the opposite side she noted a succession of similarly obvious names. The last big house had a bungalow next to it, its barren garden planted with Japanese cherries whose stark branches stuck upwards like the spokes of umbrellas turned inside out.

Beyond it there remained only a single terrace. Alice's eyebrows went up in surprise. The block of coke-dark late-Victorian houses was so out of character in this prosperous street that she could hardly believe her eyes. They were small and cramped, incongruous against the background of swelling green hills, and they reminded Alice of miners' dwellings, blackened by smoke from pit chimneys.

Each bore a stucco plate under its eaves with its name and the date, 1872. Dirt and time had obscured the lettering. To read the plate on the first house she had to come right up to the iron gate, lean over it and peer.

Alice felt a bitter let-down, a cold stab of disappointment. The house was called Kirkby. Nesta's house was going to be one of these, of course it was. But Nesta *couldn't* live here. To come to this after Salstead? Helicon Lane and The Bridal Wreath had been so exquisite. Scotch pines sheltered the little

4

shop with its steep steps and its iron railings; out of the pavement by its forecourt grew the historic Salstead Oak through whose split trunk it was said a man could ride on horseback and from whose branches mistletoe hung in a loose green ball.

She told herself not to jump to conclusions. That dark side of her character, that pessimistic side that had always been liable to fear the worst, had never manifested itself since her marriage. Andrew had taught her to be gay, frivolous almost. Stoically she looked up again. Kirkby, Garrowby, Sewerby and—yes, Revesby. So it wasn't one of these, after all. She heaved a sigh of relief.

And yet... Wasn't it rather odd to come upon four houses whose names all ended in the same way as Saulsby and Saulsby not be one of them? Perhaps there were more—prettier than these or smartened up in some way—right at the end of the road. But the houses petered out after the next fifty yards and the pavements changed to grass verges blackened with mud and diesel. In this direction the only building was Orphingham Castle, standing out grey and gaunt against a background of fast-flowing cloud. She had come to the end of the town.

'Excuse me...'

A woman in a tweed suit and mackintosh was approaching the road from a field path. She clambered heavily over a stile and came diffidently up to Alice with the suspicious look people wear when accosted by strangers.

'Can you tell me where there's a house called Saulsby?'

'In Chelmsford Road?'

'Yes, Saulsby. I can't find it anywhere.'

The woman pointed in the direction of the terrace. Under the pall of cloud the squat houses seemed to frown back. Alice frowned too.

'That's Sewerby.'

'Canvassing, are you? They do make these mistakes over names. It'll be Sewerby you want, all right.'

'I'm not canvassing. I'm going to see a friend of mine.' Alice got out her address book. 'Look, Saulsby.' Interested, the woman peered over her shoulder. 'She wrote to me and told me her address.'

'Somebody's made a mistake somewhere, if you ask me. You take my advice and ask at Sewerby.'

You take my advice... Well, she had asked for advice and she might as well take it. There was no bell on the shabby front door of Sewerby, only a knocker in the shape of a Lincoln Imp. Alice tapped and waited. For a while—half a minute perhaps—she heard nothing. Then from within there came a shambling shuffling sound. The door was bolted and the bolt squeaked as it was drawn back. It opened and she saw a very old man, as pale and purblind as if he had been shut up for years in the dark. From the dim hole of a hall came a stench of boiled cabbage, unwashed clothes and camphor.

'Good afternoon. Is Mrs Drage at home?'

'Who?'

'Mrs Drage. Mrs Nesta Drage.'

'There's only me here, lady.' He wore an ancient over-large suit and his collarless shirt was fastened at the neck by a bone stud. His face was rough and wrinkled, the skin had the texture of rind on old cheese. 'Been all on my own since the wife went,' he said. 'All on my own since fifty-four.'

'But Mrs Drage used to live here,' Alice persisted. 'A young woman, a girl really. She's very pretty with fair hair. She came here about three months ago from Salstead. I thought she had a...' She paused, realising that the standards she had set for Nesta were falling all the time. '...a room or something,' she said.

'I never let no rooms. It'll be Mrs Currie at Kirkby you want, her what's got a girl nursing at the hospital, but she only takes young fellers.'

So it wasn't Sewerby. She *had* been right. From the page in the address book she read it again: Saulsby. Nesta had written to her—written to her twice—and although she had thrown away the letters, she had copied the address down at once. It was incomprehensible, absurd.

Slowly she walked back the way she had come. The Elms, El Kantara, Beechwood, St. Andrew's, Orphingham Lodge and twenty more. But no Saulsby, no Saulsby in the whole street.

Suppose you knew the name of a house and the name of the street it was in, but you couldn't find the house, how did you go about finding it? 'Canvassing, are you?' That was it. The electoral register, the voters' list!

The police station was in the centre of the town between a public house called The Lion and Lamb and the cottage hospital. Alice went in. The station sergeant had naturally never heard of Saulsby but he provided a copy of the electoral register.

'She won't be on it,' he said, 'not if she's new here.'

But Saulsby would be. Here it was, Chelmsford Road.

'Kirkby, Garrowby, Sewerby, Revesby,' she read aloud and her voice faltered.

'She's written to you from that address, madam?'

'Of course she has, twice.'

'Well, now, I don't rightly know what to suggest.' He hesitated and then, suddenly inspired, added: 'What does she do for a living?'

'She's a florist. She used to have a flower shop in Salstead. You mean I could enquire at all the florists?'

'All two of them,' he said. 'Wouldn't do any harm, would it?'

At the first she drew a blank. The second was larger and busier. Inside the air was humid yet fresh with scent. That particular perfume, a mixture of roses, acrid chrysanthemums and the heavy languor of carnations, brought Nesta back to her as perhaps nothing else could. It seemed to go naturally with the plump pretty face, the golden hair and the common-place prattle.

The woman ahead of her was ordering wedding flowers. Back in May, when Alice and Andrew had been married, Nesta had given them all the flowers for a wedding present, sewing with her own hands the white orchid to a length of satin ribbon Alice had carried in a prayer book; early in the morning she had come to Vair Place and banked the walls of Uncle Justin's drawing-room with Whitsun Lilies.

'Do you have a Mrs Drage working for you?'

She smiled and opened her eyes in wide delight when the manageressy girl replied. 'Yes, dear. She's just gone out the back to see to an order. She won't be a minute.'

The search was over. As she waited she felt a quick little twinge of shame and of—envy? Only a woman who had never had to work for her living would come looking for a friend who did work, come on a weekday and expect to find her at home. Of course Nesta would have to work and perhaps she wouldn't be able to leave the shop for long. But then, she comforted herself, something could surely be done to persuade the manageress to let her leave early, or at least get away for a few minutes. She, Alice, could buy some-thing—she slipped her hand into her bag and felt the thick roll of notes she always carried—something ex-travagant to give to Nesta. Those orchids, possibly, or a dozen long-stemmed red roses.

'I'll give her a call, shall I? I'm sure I don't know what's keeping her.'

Alice wandered about the shop, making plans. It was going to be so good to see Nesta again. I do hope she's got over that depression, she thought. Surely the change of air and environment would have cured it by now. In a moment she would come through that door, ducking her head to avoid an ivy in a hanging basket. She would be wearing a black nylon overall and her hands would be damp, with leaf shreds ad-hering to them. A sleepy smile would cross her face, for she had always looked lately as if she had just been awakened from a disturbing dream, and she would come out with one of her characteristic, en-dearing catch-phrases.

'Well, this is a surprise. Long time no see!'

A surprise? No, she wouldn't say that, for Alice had

written to her to tell her she was coming, and in five minutes the mystery of the house that wasn't there would be cleared up.

From the back of the shop came the sound of paper being crumpled, then footsteps. Alice smiled eagerly and took a step forward.

'Nesta...'

She blinked and put her hand up to her lips.

'This lady here is Mrs Drake. Sorry to have kept you.'

The disappointment was so sharp that she felt her face muscles fall into an almost comical dismay. Her eyeballs prickled. Mrs Drake was thin, red-armed and middle-aged.

'I said Mrs *Drage*.'

'I'm sorry, I'm sure, but I could have sworn...'

She shook her head and turned her back on them. So much frustration was past bearing. She stood on the pavement in the rain, the umbrella dangling from her wrist like a wet deflated pod, staring drearily at the shoppers. Nesta might be among them. Surely...? She started, looking again, and began to run after the little figure in the black shiny raincoat whose bright hair was escaping under a scarf. But as she put out her hand to touch the sleeve the woman turned and showed a pig's face with rosy corrugated skin and scarlet lips.

A sob rose in her throat and with it the beginning of panic. It was an old familiar feeling, this sudden fear, this dread of something terrible about to happen. Familiar but old, half-forgotten in the happiness of the past year. Calm, practical, matter-of-fact. That, she knew, was how everyone thought of her.

Suddenly she felt very young, almost childish. She wanted to cry and she wanted Andrew. Strange, because the two impulses were incompatible. In his eyes she was strong, calm and maternal. With a little catch of her breath she turned and caught sight of herself in the rain-dashed glass of a shop window, a tall substantial woman with broad shoulders made to cry on, not to shake with sobs.

Nesta had often cried on them. When you are young and pretty you can cry and nobody minds, nobody reprimands you. Why think of that now? Pull yourself together, she told herself in another of Nesta's clichés. She lifted her sleeve and glanced at the little platinum and diamond watch. Almost four. In an hour's time Hugo and Jackie would come looking for Nesta's house, driving up and down the street, growing angrier and more impatient. She could hardly sit on the wall outside Sewerby, waiting for them in the pouring rain. It was almost funny when you thought of it like that, not a crying matter at all.

In all her thirty-eight years Alice had hardly ever used a public telephone box. For communication with its outlying villages Orphingham had a complicated dialling system, a series of codes. What was the name of the firm whose factory Hugo was visiting? He had only mentioned it once. Amalgamated something—paints, varnishes, sprays. . . . She opened the directory and found it quickly. Amalgamated Lacquers, Orph Bridge. Away from Salstead and the people she had known all her life, Alice was always a little ill-at-ease, uncertain, shy. Never having had to make her own way in the world, she was daunted by the unfamiliar. Tentatively she studied the code and worked the dial slowly. Outside it was beginning to grow dark. Water drummed on the roof and washed down the glass walls.

'May I speak to Mrs. Whittaker, please?'

She found she had to explain more fully than that. There followed clicks and trills as someone worked a switchboard, then Jackie's puzzled, slightly apprehensive voice.

'Hallo? Is that you, Mummy?'

'It's Alice.'

'Oh God! I thought there was something wrong with the kids. What's the matter?'

Alice told her. In the background she could hear voices, restrained laughter.

'You've obviously made a mistake,' Jackie said rather sharply. 'Got the address wrong. Have you got her letters with you?'

'I haven't got them at all. I threw them away.'

'Well, there you are, then. You got the address mixed up.'

'That's not possible, Jackie. Nesta left a ring at Cropper's to have it enlarged. I sent it to her at Saulsby and I sent letters too. She got the ring, she wrote to me and thanked me for it. She even sent two pounds to cover the cost of the enlargement.'

'You mean you sent letters and a parcel to a place that doesn't exist and you got answers?' Jackie's tone was gentler now, yet high-pitched with a sort of excitement. 'Listen, I'll come over and fetch you and then we'll come back for Hugo.'

'Now, let's see. She moved away from Salstead at the beginning of August and she was very vague about where she was going. She said she hadn't got anything fixed but she'd write and let you know when she was settled. Right?'

Alice nodded. 'I didn't like to bother her with a lot of questions, Jackie. She'd been so depressed lately. She'd been in Salstead three years at that shop and she said that was enough. It can't be much fun being a widow and having to earn your own living. She's so young.'

'Young!' Jackie stretched her trousered legs. 'She's older than I am. Twenty-eight if she's a day.' She added thoughtfully: 'A cross between a Jersey cow and a china doll, that's how she struck me.'

That was not at all how Nesta had struck Alice. Looking back to a couple of years before she was married, she remembered how she had gone into The

Bridal Wreath when it had first come under Nesta's management. The wreaths of variegated laurel and the pots of solanum sprouting little orange balls had all been taken away and replaced by specie fuchsias and orchids in green metal trays. In her slow dreamy way Nesta had loved orchids. Their gleaming opaque flesh seemed to have an affinity with her own, their petals curved and pearly like her nails. Alice recaptured that first sight of her now, in one of the black dresses she always wore, the only brightness about her pale vivid hair, stacked and interwoven into a filagree cone.

'It was about a month after she moved that I went into Cropper's to get that watch for Andrew. Nesta had taken her engagement ring in to have it enlarged—'

'I'm not surprised,' Jackie interrupted. 'She was putting on weight like mad. I noticed the way her ankles absolutely bulged when she tottered about in those crazy high heels.'

'Anyway, she must have forgotten to collect the ring before she left. I told Mr Cropper I'd send it to her, but I didn't know her address.'

'Was that when you were going to put an advertisement in *The Times*?'

'I knew Nesta wouldn't read *The Times*, but I thought she might have a friend or a relative who would. I was still thinking about it when I had a letter from her. It was just a couple of lines, but I sent the ring and she wrote back and thanked me for it. But that's weeks and weeks ago now.'

From the scuffed handbag of tooled leather she always carried Jackie took a packet of Sobranie Cocktail cigarettes, selected a pale green one and lit it reflectively. The smoke curled up to the car roof like a feather or a branching flower. 'How could she have got the ring if you sent it to a place that isn't there?'

'I don't know,' said Alice.

Above them the rain pattered rhythmically. The sound it made was like the regular tap-tap of little scurrying heels or long-nailed fingers drumming nervously on metal.

'You'd better tidy yourself up a bit,' Jackie said as she started the car. 'You look as if you've got caught in a storm on a cross-country run.'

A year before Alice would have resented the remark. Now she only smiled. 'I'll never be a glamour queen.'

'A *glamour* queen? Where do you get these expressions, out of the ark?'

'I don't need to—to attract people. I've got a husband.'

'Your Andrew,' said Jackie slyly, 'is a very attractive man.'

'I know.'

'I always think dark men are much more sexy than fair men, don't you?'

'Oh, Jackie, I've never thought about it.'

'Well, you can take it from me, they are. Frankly, lovey—I know you won't mind my saying this, you're too sensible, aren't you?—frankly I've often wondered how you managed to catch Andrew in the first place. Picked him up at some tinpot school sports, didn't you?'

'It wasn't a school sports, it was Founder's Day. And I didn't pick him up. I went with a friend whose little boy was at school there. We were talking to the English master. . . .'

'And the English master was Andrew.'

'Jackie, dear, I thought every Whittaker in the place knew the story by now. We wrote to each other and had dinner together. Isn't that how most women meet their husbands?'

'I met Hugo in a pub.'

'Yes, I remember, but for goodness' sake don't let Uncle Justin know.'

Jackie giggled. When they were about a mile out of Orphingham she took a left-hand turn down a recently concreted lane. The factory where Hugo was resembled a great fungoid growth, plaster white and rubbery looking among the fields. Presently he came out to the car. His manner was ebullient if slightly nervous and he launched at once into an account of the contract he assured them was 'in the bag'.

'Who cares anyway?' said Jackie truculently.

'It's your bread and butter, isn't it? And Alice's, come to that. Shove over, you'd better let me drive. All you lot, you batten on Whittaker's like a bunch of parasites.' He gave an irascible grunt. Jackie lit a blue cigarette, elaborately calm. Hugo sniffed. 'Give me one, will you? Not one of those, a real cigarette. Couldn't care less about the works, could you?' All the Whittakers referred to their factory as 'the works'. 'Never think about it, do you? Grasshoppers living it up while the ants do all the work, the ants being Justin and me.' He grunted again. 'Oh, and Andrew of course,' he added as an afterthought and as a sop to Alice.

She was used to his quick gusts of temper, spurts

of rage that evaporated quickly and usually meant nothing. 'I'm sorry Jackie had to come back,' she said peaceably, 'but I suppose you've gathered that I couldn't find Nesta. The house just wasn't there.'

'What d'you mean, wasn't there? Oh, damn and blast him!' He braked sharply, stuck his head out in the rain and shouted at the driver of a molasses tanker. The traffic was dense, a glittering sluggish caterpillar.

'It's useless trying to talk to you,' said Jackie. She gasped and exclaimed suddenly, 'Why didn't we think of it? We should have gone to the Post Office.' The car jerked almost into the tanker's tail lights and the big sign attached to its rear, *Caution*, *Air Brakes*, seemed to leap against the window-screen. 'Hugo!' she screamed. 'What the hell are you doing? Will you still love me when I've had plastic surgery?'

'Oh, Jackie,' said Alice miserably, 'I wish I'd thought of the Post Office. It was the obvious place. I went to the police, but I never thought. . . .'

'You went to the *police*?' Hugo sounded aghast.

'Only for the voter's list. Could we go back, Hugo? It's worrying me rather.'

'Go back? It'd worry me rather if I had to go back through this hell's delight in the middle of the rush. Besides, they'll be closed.'

'I suppose so. I didn't think.'

In fact it was difficult to see how anyone could turn and go back. The crawling queue remained unbroken and serpentine all the way to the Brentwood fork. Then one in three trickled away.

'Thank God this'll be a thing of the past when the by-pass opens next week.'

The whole stream came to a shivering stop as the first cars edged into the bottleneck of Salstead High Street. To her right Alice could see the white mouth of the twin-track road and across it a row of oil drums set about with red warning lights. The new lamps were in place but unlighted. It was a ghost road, a virgin stretch of concrete over which no tyre had yet passed. Still and silent, it dwindled away between dark embankments of piled-up clay. Alice could just make out the big flat direction sign in the distance and the acute-angled branch where the slip road forked away to meet the High Street in the centre of the town. On the other side of that slip road lay Helicon Lane. It was a stump now, its lower end lopped off to allow the passage of the bypass, but The Bridal Wreath was still there, the oak and the swinging mistletoe....

At the cross roads they left the High Street and turned down Station Road. The lights were on in the doctor's surgery and Mr Cropper was veiling his window display in the metal night guard that looked like a curtain of chain mail. At any rate, Nesta had got her ring. Somewhere in the elusive Saulsby she might even now be slipping it on above her wedding ring, twisting it and smiling as the light caught the facets of the diamond chips.

People were going into The Boadicea. It must be gone six. The car sped smoothly between new developments of semi-detached houses, under the railway bridge, past 'the works'—Whittaker-Hinton, est. 1856. The last of the workers were leaving, in cars, on bicycles, some on foot. Hugo slowed, raising his hand in salute, and Alice recognised his secretary coming down the steps. Uncle Justin's Bentley and Andrew's Sprite were missing from the executives' car park. The car moved on quickly into the peace of the wet sequestered countryside.

Vair House was much smaller than Vair Place, but built at the same period and of the same tulip-red bricks, and it clung close to its side without being joined to it. It was rather as if the parent building had actually given birth to Vair House, had delivered a child unmistakably its own, though not its replica.

The larger house topped the others by perhaps a dozen feet and this extra space consisted of an overhanging roof from which four dormers protruded. From these windows, and indeed from all the upper windows of both houses, an unscarred view was to be had of Salstead's outlying meadows. Justin Whittaker, who lived at Vair Place, said that just as there was nothing ugly or incongruous about what he called the demesne, so nothing unsightly was visible from it.

Even the new service station on the Pollington Road was concealed by a fine wall of limes, whitebeams and larches. Only St Jude's spire could be seen, a tenuous needle of stone above a web of branches. By building their factory just outside the station the Whittakers had for ever ruined the visitor's first prospect of Salstead; their own dwelling they had taken care to guard from depredations.

Alice and Hugo, orphaned as children, had been brought up by their father's brother, the present head of the firm. But when Hugo married he had chosen to build himself a new bungalow a quarter of a mile away. Vair House fell vacant when the last Hinton aunt died and had remained so until Uncle Justin gave it to Alice on her marriage to Andrew.

Andrew... It was just the place for him, she thought as Hugo dropped her at the entrance to the drive and she began to walk towards the house. She could hardly remember anything that had given her greater pleasure than that first day she had shown him Vair House and had told him it was to be their home instead of one of the stucco-fronted bungalows reserved for married masters at Pudsey School. Unless—unless it was giving him the little red Sprite for a wedding present or the gold watch on his birthday or the William and Mary bookcase for his Trollope first editions.

The Sprite was on the drive now, dwarfed by Uncle Justin's Bentley on the other side of the hedge. Of course, he would be home by now. Alice looked at her watch. Almost half past six. She rounded the only bend in the path and then she saw him waiting for her to come.

She knew he was waiting for her although he was not looking into the garden. The curtains had not yet been drawn and through the small square panes she could see the pink light from one of the lamps falling on his face and on the book he was reading. As she came up the steps, tiptoeing because she loved to come upon him unawares, she could see every detail of the cameo in the embrasure of the window: Andrew's long hands that always reminded her of the hands in Titian's *L'homme au Gant*, the signet ring on his finger, even the cover of one of his favourite Palliser novels, brown and duck-egg blue with the Huskinson drawing.

She let herself in quietly. In front of the hall glass she paused and looked at herself. When she had married and brought Andrew to Salstead she had made a firm resolution. Nothing about her appearance should be changed. Let them laugh and gossip because dowdy Alice Whittaker had found herself a husband at last—and what a husband! They would have laughed and talked more, she thought, if she had taken to wearing high heels and short skirts and had had her hair cut.

In the great hall at Pudsey she had looked the way she always did, a woman with a splendid figure—a fine woman, Andrew said—in a Macclesfield silk dress and sensible low-heeled sandals, her hair done in the way it had been since she had first put up the plaits when she was seventeen. Andrew had spoken to her, sat with her, fallen in love with her just the way she was. Why should she change?

Still... She remembered Jackie's reproaches and felt a tiny stab of doubt. The scarf might look better draped against the neck of her sweater with the brooch pinned to it, or knotted perhaps. She fumbled unsuccessfully; then, smiling at her small vanities, discarded the scarf and fastened the brooch again. Behind her the door swung and she knew he was standing there. His face appeared in the glass over her shoulder.

'"She well knew",' he quoted, laughing, '"the great architectural secret of decorating a construction and never descended to construct a decoration."'

'Darling Andrew!'

'I was beginning to get worried about you.'

He put out his arms and she went into them, just as if they had been parted for a month.

'You weren't really worried?'

'I would have been if you hadn't come soon. Hungry?' She nodded. 'I sent Pernille off to the pictures. Apparently some early gem of Bergman has found its way to the Pollington Plaza. She'll be back in time to get dinner.'

He followed her into the drawing-room. The tea things were arranged on a low table with thin bread and butter and pastries from the cake shop in York Street.

'I waited tea for you.'

'Waited? Oh, Andrew, you got all this ready specially, didn't you?'

'*Madame est servie.*'

The fire was just beginning to come up. She imagined him letting it die down, not noticing. Then, when it was six o'clock and still she hadn't come, rushing to pile logs on the ashes. She warmed her hands at the thin yellow flames, remembering the first time he had ever handed her a cup of tea in the hall at Pudsey on Founder's Day.

He too had felt it or read her thoughts, for he said gravely, 'Do you take milk, Miss Whittaker?'

She laughed, lifting her face to his and meeting there a shared tenderness, an awareness of the miracle that had happened to them both. It was still impossible for her to believe that he loved her as much as she loved him, yet impossible to doubt when she saw in his eyes that glow of wonder and delight. Love had come to her late and unlooked for. 'It's so romantic,' Nesta had sighed, 'it makes me want to cry,' and her pale blue eyes had filled with tears. Nesta might be crying somewhere now because she had waited for Alice and Alice had failed to come. She drew away from Andrew, keeping hold of his hand. If Nesta had really been waiting for her, surely she would have telephoned.

'Tell me what you've been doing,' she said. 'Anything happened, anyone phoned?'

'Harry Blunden came in, ostensibly to lend me something and to return a book he'd borrowed. You see, he's torn the cover.' He shrugged, indicating a long rent in the jacket of the novel he had been reading. 'He's a ham-handed character for a doctor. I hope he never has to give me an injection.'

So Nesta, wherever she was, had kept silence and was content to do so. 'I haven't seen Harry for weeks and weeks,' she said. Harry might know, he had been Nesta's doctor. 'What did you mean, ostensibly?'

'Of course, he really came to see you, Bell.' He always called her Bell, for it was the Victorian diminutive of her second Christian name. 'I shall call you Bell,' he had said when she had told him she was called Alice Christabel. 'Alice is too hard for you. Alice is for old spinsters, not young wives. . . .'

'What did Harry want?'

He laughed. 'Just to see you, I imagine. He hung about flapping his great hands for half an hour, more or less tongue-tied, and then he had to take his evening surgery.'

'You don't like Harry, do you?'

'Naturally I don't like men who are in love with my wife,' he said lightly. 'I don't like men who treat her house as if it were a shrine and I don't like men who make a point of sitting in her favourite chair because they know she sat there last. He carries his torch aloft over the ground you tread on.' Smiling a little, he sat down on the floor at her feet. 'Which age-old platitudes,' he said, 'bring me to your friend Nesta. How was she? Tell me all about it.'

'There's nothing to tell. I didn't see her. It's awfully odd, darling, but I couldn't find her.'

'What d'you mean, Bell?' He listened in silence, relaxed and perfectly still, as she told him about it.

'What did you say the house was called?'

She took a pastry basket full of marzipan fruit and bit into it.

'Saulsby. I know Jackie thinks I've got it wrong, but I haven't. It's in my book. Wait a minute and I'll get it.'

'Don't get up now. I know you don't make mistakes like that.' He shifted comfortably, looking up at her. 'You really have the most delightful cushiony lap I ever rested my head in.'

'Have you rested it in many?'

'Hundreds.'

She smiled at that, pitying the other women that had been rejected when she was chosen. 'What ought I to do about Nesta?'

'Do? Why should you do anything?'

'It seems so strange.'

'There's probably some quite simple explanation.'

'I hope so. I can't help feeling she may be in some kind of trouble. Do you remember how depressed and strange she was when she left?'

'I remember she went around saying good-bye to everyone, metaphorically rattling her collecting box.'

'Oh, darling!'

'She foisted herself on us because she said everything was packed up for the move and she couldn't cook herself a meal.'

'Pernille was ill so I had to cook it, but the cheese soufflé went flat and it was ghastly.'

'It wasn't particularly ghastly,' he said, and added teasingly: 'You should have invited Harry as well. I'm sure he'd guzzle. . . .' He paused, selecting the worst thing he could think of. '. . . chocolate-coated ants if he thought you'd cooked them.'

'Horrible!' Alice shuddered. 'And then she had one of her little weeps,' she went on, 'and you drove her back to The Bridal Wreath. Goodness knows why because she was going to spend the night with the Feasts. That was the first night they began moving the old graves to make room for the slip road. Nesta had a thing about it.'

'The uncontrolled imagination of the ill-educated,' Andrew said pompously. He grinned at her.

'Don't be so unkind. Even you wouldn't have been awfully keen on sleeping a hundred yards from where a lot of people were unearthing corpses. I know I wouldn't. They even had a policeman and the vicar there and I think that made it worse. But she wasn't there, anyway. I do wish I knew where she is now, Andrew.'

'Bell?' He sat up suddenly. 'Could we give Nesta Drage a rest?'

She looked at him questioningly.

'I was glad when she went away,' he said. 'I never

have been able to see what you saw in her, Bell.
When you said she'd borrowed money off you—I
didn't like that.' When she began to protest he went
on soothingly: 'All right, she paid it back. Today when
you went to Orphingham I confess I thought you'd
come back several hundred pounds poorer and a
partner in another hopeless bit of private enterprise
like the last one. But you didn't see her. Darling, I'm
not much of a one for signs and portents, but I can't
help seeing this mixup over addresses as the interpo-
sition of a kindly Providence.'

'I was going to go back to Orphingham tomorrow.'

'I wouldn't if I were you.' She had never been
clever at concealing her thoughts. Now she felt disappointment must show in every feature, for he said
impulsively, 'You're really worried about this, aren't
you?'

She nodded.

He sat back on his heels and, taking both her
hands, smiled at her tenderly. 'I'm so afraid you'll be
hurt. Why not wait till Saturday and then I can come
with you?'

'Oh, Andrew, I don't need a bodyguard!'

He was still looking at her with that strange mixture of solicitude and amusement. 'Not a bodyguard,'
he said, and his voice held a kind of sad intensity.
'There are other kinds of vulnerability.'

'Sticks and stones,' she said lightly. 'You know how
it goes on.'

'Perhaps the most insensitive proverb of them all,
certainly the most obtuse.'

Alice went upstairs to dress. It was absurd of Andrew to be so protective. If any of her relatives had

heard him they would hardly have been able to keep from laughing, knowing how strong and self-sufficient she was. Maternal was the word they used to describe her, a fit adjective for a woman who had married a man nine years younger than herself.

ʃʃʃʃʃʃʃʃʃʃʃʃʃʃʃʃʃʃʃ **3** ʃʃʃʃʃʃ

'AND WHERE,' ASKED UNCLE JUSTIN AS HE GOT
out of the Bentley, 'do you think you're going? Why
aren't you having your luncheon?'

He came towards the hedge and looked her up and
down. What he saw must have displeased him, for he
gave no hint of a smile.

Alice recalled that some wit had once said of the
family that all the Whittakers looked like the
descendants of a monstrous union between a golden
cocker and an Arab mare, but that only the males
favoured the distaff side. Certainly Justin Whittaker
looked very like a horse. His forehead was low but
saved from ignobility by its width. The distance between his eyes and his mouth was great and made
illusorily greater by the deep parallel lines which his
constantly compressed lips had cut from his nose to
his chin. His large teeth were all his own but he sel-

dom showed them, keeping his underlip in a position of what he called determination, others pugnacity.

'I'm going to the starvation lunch, Uncle Justin, the bread and cheese lunch for Oxfam,' said Alice bravely, remembering that she was a married woman now. 'They have one every Friday.'

'Roman Catholic rubbish.'

It was useless to argue with him. Better for him to think she was toying with the Church of Rome than for him to fling at her his most opprobrious taunt, 'Socialist!'

'You don't have to pay for it, do you?'

'Of course we pay for it. That's the point.' She drew a deep breath. 'The proceeds go to Oxfam. I told you. At the moment we're trying to raise enough to buy agricultural machinery for an Indian village.'

He frowned, shaking his head. His silver tie was always so tightly knotted that he had to hold his chin up.

'I wonder what you think we're going to do with all these people you're feeding on the fat of the land. You aren't going to like it, Alice, when they come over here and live in prefabs all over Vair.'

'I can't argue now, Uncle Justin, I'll be late.'

'A lot of old tabbies, I suppose.' His look indicated that he included her among them, not a real woman, a pretty woman. Women in his view should be seen, and should be worth seeing, but should seldom be heard. 'You don't get any men there, I'm sure.'

'Yes, we do.' Alice owned to herself that he was almost right, and then named the only four men who ever attended. 'Mr Feast from the dairy—he's the treasurer—and Harry Blunden often comes. The vicar's almost always there and Father Mulligan from Our Lady of Fatima.'

'There you are, what did I say? You'd much better come and eat your luncheon with me.'

She was almost tempted. Lunch at Vair Place was delightful. She pictured her uncle eating the meal that seldom varied. A small glass of Manzanilla always preceded it, then came a steak and apple pie cooked by Mrs Johnson and served by Kathleen. His version of bread and cheese was Thin Wine Biscuits and a triangle of Camembert.

'I must go,' she said. 'Don't forget you're having dinner with us tonight.'

It was now much too late to walk. By the time she had battled through the lunchtime traffic and found a place to park she saw that it was a quarter past one. But the pitch pine of St Jude's hall was still hopefully open.

The hall floor was covered with light brown lino that, because it was never polished, looked like milk chocolate that has been left too long exposed to the air. At a trestle table just inside the door, a table laden with collecting boxes and hung with posters, sat a very thin man. He was even more emaciated than the starved children who, with distended bellies and feverish eyes, stared hopelessly from the flapping photographs.

'I'm sorry I'm late, Mr Feast.' Alice had known him too long to be amused by or even to notice the incongruity of his name.

'Better late than never.' In his throat a huge bulge, like an Adam's Apple swollen to monstrous proportions, stuck out above his collar. It was the only prominent thing about him. If only, Andrew had once proposed, he could be induced to stand at the hall entrance in a loincloth even Uncle Justin's hostility to the cause would melt. The most reactionary would join the bread and cheese eaters, perhaps unaware of the true objects of their fast.

She passed on quickly.

'Good morning, Miss Whit—Mrs Fielding, I should say,' said the vicar. He had married her but it would take him more than six months to get over the habit of twenty years. 'We haven't seen as much of you lately as we should like.' It was the very phrase he used to church backsliders.

I have married a husband and therefore I cannot come, Alice nearly said. Instead she smiled. 'Well, I'm here now.'

'Yes, indeed, and most welcome.'

He led her to one of the long deal tables and hesitated between the many empty chairs. Her eyes travelled from the oil painting of James Whittaker, builder of this hall, splendid in frock coat, watch and chain, to the different pictures beneath. Under each piously Gothic window hung a poster of a hungry child with an empty bowl, so that from where she stood it seemed as if a queue of malnourished infants stretched the length of the hall, watching and waiting.

'Alice! Come and have a place in the sun.' Harry Blunden pushed back his bentwood chair and stood up. 'Here you are, the warmest place in the room.'

She smiled up into his lean ugly face, trying not to

show the embarrassment she felt when she saw in his blue eyes so much naked love.

'Thank you, Harry.'

His extreme height had always been a nuisance to him—she imagined him ducking beneath hospital bed curtains, bending almost double over the sick— that he now had a permanent stoop. 'There, what's it going to be?' He eased her coat from her shoulders. 'Mousetrap or best-quality kitchen soap?' It was the no longer funny remark he always made when they met at the Friday lunch.

'Oh, mousetrap. But please not that bit with the evil-looking hole in it.'

The table was covered with a cloth of white plastic. There were bread rolls and rough-hewn chunks of French stick all tumbled together in Pyrex bowls, cheese in bricks as dry and unappetising as the wood of the table, and, in a jam-jar, a small bunch of attenuated watercress. Everyone had a plate, a knife and a Woolworth glass tumbler.

'Hallo, Mrs Fielding.'

Alice looked across the table and met the eyes of a thin girl with long shaggy hair that reached to her shoulder blades.

'Hallo, Daphne. You're the very person I wanted to see.'

Daphne Feast parted the strands of hair and peered at her.

'I know. I've been talking to your sister-in-law.'

'*Jackie*? Is Jackie *here*?'

Reaching a long arm rudely across the plate of a plump woman sitting two places from her, Daphne pointed to the far end of the table where Jackie sat between her two small children.

'She said you'd been looking for Nesta Drage. She'd given you a false address or something.'

'Well, it wasn't quite—' Alice stopped as Harry interrupted her. She wished he wouldn't always try to monopolise her.

'Gave you a false address?' he said. 'But you went to see her, didn't you?'

'Yes, I did, but...'

She lifted up her glass as the vicar approached their section of the table with a jug of water.

'How much do we have to pay for this?' asked the plump woman suspiciously.

The vicar beamed. 'Just whatever you would have paid for your normal lunch at home.'

'But I don't have any lunch at home! My mother-in-law won't let me. She says if I put on any more weight I'll get a coronary, I won't get a coronary, will I, Dr Blunden?'

Harry turned towards her reluctantly. 'Just as well to be on the safe side,' he said.

'I wish you'd come and sit by me, Doctor, and tell me what I ought to do so that I can tell my mother-in-law.'

Alice could see he didn't want to move. For a moment he hesitated. Then he got up and smiling abstractedly, walked around the table carrying his plate.

'I thought you might know where Nesta really is,' she said to Daphne. 'You were such close friends.'

'Oh, I don't know. We used to have a bit of a giggle together. That's all.'

'Didn't she tell you where she was going either? She must have given you an address to write to.'

'She knew I'd never write, Mrs Fielding. We were —what'd you call it—ships that pass in the night. She never even said a proper good-bye, but I'm not breaking my heart over it.'

Alice was bewildered. 'But she stayed with you and your father on her last night. August the seventh, that Friday night. She had supper with us and then she went to stay with you.'

'She never turned up.'

'I thought it was a definite arrangement.'

'Not what you'd call an arrangement. She did *say* she'd come and Pop and me waited for her, but there was a play on the telly and what with her having the phone cut off I couldn't get in touch with her. You know how it is.'

No, she didn't know. She wrote down all her engagements in a twin to the big address book and she had never failed to keep a coffee-morning date, let alone breaking a promise to spend the night in a friend's house.

'Didn't you go round to The Bridal Wreath to find out?'

The suggestion almost seemed to shock Daphne. She nibbled at her last fragment of cheese. 'I told you, there was this play on. Pop just went up to The Boadicea for a beer and I said, "Keep your eyes open for Nesta," but he never had sight nor sound of her. When it got to ten I gave her up.' She leaned confidingly across the table. 'Quite frankly, Mrs Fielding, I didn't go much on going down Helicon Lane in the dark, not with all those graves being turned up.'

Heavens! Alice gave herself a little shake. There was something ghoulish about Daphne's pallid face in which only the eyes were made up, the streaming hair that trailed across the bread bowl.

'Well,' she said, 'it's a mystery, isn't it? Before I sent the ring off to Nesta—when I didn't know anything of her whereabouts—I asked everyone in Salstead who knew her and no one had her address.'

'You asked me then,' said Daphne mournfully, 'and I asked Pop and all the shop people.'

On the other side of the table Harry looked as if his patience was being exhausted. The plump woman's voice rang out, 'I suppose there's nothing to stop me going into The Boadicea when I've finished this and having a proper lunch, is there?'

'On your own head be it,' said Harry. He came round behind Alice's chair, stopped and patted her shoulder. 'I wouldn't do too much of this, if I were you, Alice.' His voice had dropped and she swivelled round quickly because his words were plainly intended only for her ears, 'You need proper meals. You've been looking tired lately.'

'But I feel fine.'

The words were almost a whisper and she had to strain to catch them. 'If there's even anything troubling you—*anything*, Alice, you'll come to me, won't you?'

'You know I'm never ill, Harry.'

He shook his head, increased the pressure of his hand and then withdrew it. Puzzled, she watched him cross to the table where Mr Feast sat taking the money. Harry was a doctor, *her* doctor. Why then had she received such a strong impression that the trouble he feared for her wasn't physical at all?

'You said it was a mystery,' said Daphne Feast. 'Well, I'll tell you something. There were a lot of mysteries about Nesta.'

At the hint of gossip Alice felt herself shrinking. All she wanted was to find out where Nesta was and why she was hiding herself.

'For one thing she was involved with some man.'

'Oh, come!' Nesta had been devoted to the memory of her dead husband, even to the extent of still wearing mourning three years after his death. One day certainly she would get married again. Anyone as pretty as she was bound to. But, involved with a man? Nesta had been lonely and forlorn. It was because of this and in an effort to save her from the company of people like the Feasts that Alice had made a point of cultivating her.

'She wouldn't tell me who he was,' Daphne said firmly, 'only that he was a big man in Salstead and that some people would have a bit of a shock when it came out.' She lit a cigarette and dropped the match among the crusts and cheese rinds on her plate. 'I reckon he was married. There was some reason he didn't want it known. Nesta said he'd have to marry her one of these fine days. We had a bit of a giggle about it.'

'That sounds like day-dreaming to me,' said Alice severely.

'There was another funny thing. Nothing to do with her love life, but a funny thing.' Daphne flicked her ash across the table.

I'm not surprised Nesta didn't want to stay with the Feasts, Alice thought.

'Did you ever notice her eyebrows?'

'Her *eyebrows*?'

'You think I'm daft, don't you? No, you wouldn't have noticed, not with her being so neurotic about the way she looked. Well, when she first came here she had thick sort of fair eyebrows and very long lashes. Right?'

Yes, Nesta had beautiful eyebrows and long soft lashes. Her blonde hair had been abundant too.

'Well, naturally she used to pluck her eyebrows, but one day she was a bit heavy-handed and she pulled too much out. She said she'd have to let them grow...'

'Well?'

'Well, they never did. That's all. They never did and she used to have to sort of pencil them in. I popped into her flat once—she didn't know I was coming and, God, she jumped out of her skin—she'd taken her make-up off and she hadn't any eyebrows at all. I can tell you, Mrs Fielding, it gave me the creeps. Just eyes she had and then nothing till her hair started.'

Daphne, Alice thought, had missed her vocation. She would have made a startling impact on filmgoers as a kind of female Boris Karloff. First the graves and now this.

'Her eyelashes were—well, they were quite luxuri-ant.'

'False,' said Daphne Feast. 'I'm not kidding.'

So poor Nesta had had alopecia. Horrible, when you remembered how proud she had been of her appearance.

'Thanks, Daphne. I expect she'll turn up.'

She began to put on her gloves.

'When you do root her out you might tell her to come and collect her stuff?'

'Her stuff?'

'She got Snows to fetch round some stuff of hers the day before she left. I reckon it was a load of junk or some of those kids' jigsaw puzzles she was so crazy on doing. Anyway, you can tell her I'm fed-up with it cluttering the place up.'

'I'll tell her.'

The trouble with being a Whittaker was that everybody expected you to dispense largesse wherever you went. Glad that Uncle Justin would never know the extent of her generosity, Alice took two pound notes from her wallet and laid them on the table in front of Mr Feast.

'Quite a good—' She had nearly said 'audience,' '—attendance here today, Mr Feast.'

He began mournfully on a long diatribe. 'Always the upper crust and the working class, though you'll notice, Mrs Fielding. The bourgeoisie keep their feet under their own fat tables. That's why I've always said and always shall say, the Popular Front's an impossibility. The upper crust and the working class—'

'Do tell me, Mr Feast, which do I come in?' At Jackie's voice, Alice turned. 'I didn't know what to do with the brats so I brought them along to see how the other half lived.'

Alice bent down and swung the three-year-old up into her arms. 'He's getting heavy, Jackie! What did you think of your funny old dinner, darling?'

Her nephew flung his arms around her neck. 'I'm partial to cheese, aren't I, Mum?'

'Partial?'

'It's his latest word. Put him down, Alice. You'll strain yourself.'

'I've just made up my mind,' Alice said. 'I'm going back to Orphingham. Now. This afternoon.'

'And we're coming with you,' said Mark and Christopher together.

Smiling, Alice squatted in front of them.

'Would you like to? You can. I'd love some nice jolly company.'

'Well, you've had that for a start,' said Jackie. 'You're coming to the dentist with me.'

As the double wail went up she put her hands over her ears.

'It's a pity you haven't got any of your own, Alice. If you'd got married ten years ago you'd have had kids and all the jolly company you wanted.'

Ten years ago Andrew had been nineteen, in his second year at Cambridge. Alice wondered if Jackie knew what she had said, but although she felt the blood mounting in her own cheeks there was no sign of embarrassment on her sister-in-law's face. Jackie and Hugo, Uncle Justin all of them, only thought of Andrew's luck, the sudden rapid step he had taken into affluence. They never considered what he had lost by marrying a woman on the verge of middle age.

She took a hand of each of the boys. 'If you're very grownup about going to the dentist, I promise I'll have something lovely for you at Vair. You get Mummy to bring you at—let me see—half past five.'

'That's a vicious circle,' said Jackie. 'Fill their beastly little fangs and then rot them all over again.'

Alice walked out into the cold sunlight. If she made haste and started at once she would be in Orphingham by three.

4

THE POST OFFICE WAS CROWDED. ALICE HAD TO push her way in past prams and tethered dogs. Behind the rail on the counter top, three people were serving, a thin young man with a face so pale as to be almost green, a plump woman and another man, older and dignified, with a heavy grey moustache. Alice glanced ruefully at a legend on a poster: 'Someone, somewhere, wants a letter from you.' She joined the shortest of the queues. It was moving very slowly. Pension books were brought out and presented with dogged patience, secreted once more in bags and wallets.

'Next, please.'

'I've been sending letters to a house in Chelmsford Road,' Alice began. 'To a friend of mine. But when I went to Chelmsford Road yesterday I couldn't find the house.' Behind her an old woman pushed forward to listen. 'The name of the house is Saulsby, but there isn't a Saulsby in the whole street.'

'You mean your letters have gone astray?' The young man's voice was rough with impatience. He kept his head bent while he rummaged in a drawer. 'If they've been wrongly addressed they'll be returned to sender in due course. It's a wise precaution to put your own address....'

'I don't think they can have gone astray. I've been getting replies.'

At last he looked at her. 'You don't want us at all, do you? What you want is the council offices. They'll let you have a street plan. Next please?'

Standing her ground, Alice said desperately: 'I know the name of the street. I told you, it's Chelmsford Road. I'm sorry if you're busy...'

'Always busy on a Friday afternoon on account of everybody coming in then because it gets so crowded on Saturday.'

His lack of logic almost defeated her. She stepped back and immediately an arm in moth-eaten ocelot thrust across her and laid a pension book on the counter.

'Isn't there anyone I could talk to about this? Surely there must be someone who would know?'

'If you'd like to line up over there you could have a word with Mr Robson. He's the postmaster.'

To join Mr Robson's queue she had to go right back to the door. She counted fifteen people waiting while the postmaster served a woman in an orange sari. Five minutes passed and nobody moved. The Indian woman was buying half a dozen stamps of each denomination to send home to a philatelic relative in Calcutta. The queue began to mutter and shuffle.

Suppose I were to go back there just once more, Alice thought, and make another check on those house names now it isn't raining. Ignoring the queue, she walked straight up to the pale man's counter. 'Will it be less crowded if I come back later?'

'Pardon?'

'If I come back later?'

'You can come back later if you like.' Counting notes, he hardly bothered to look at her. 'It gets a bit slacker about half-five.'

'Do you mind not going out of your turn?' asked a tired young woman carrying a child.

Alice went back to her car and drove up the High Street to the Chelmsford Road turning. Even under the wintry sky the place had the higgledy-piggledy typically English prettiness of a calendar or a Christmas card. The townspeople evidently took pride in their rainbow variety of painted front doors, lime-washed walls and sanded steps. This place, she thought, but without malice or contempt, would have made a particular appeal to Nesta's snobbishness and her love of beauty kept within orderly bounds. Its residents could turn up their noses at certain utilitarian workaday aspects of Salstead.

Chelmsford Road was deserted. Dead chestnut leaves like ancient wrinkled hands, brown and crepitating, rustled in the gutters. None of the houses had numbers and none was called Saulsby. She walked up one side examining name plates and down the other.

The only sound to disturb the cathedral-like hush

came from the front path of El Kantara where a woman was sweeping leaves. The round-topped gate in the wall was open and just inside was a sign which read:

Orphingham Hospital Management Committee, Nurses' Home.

'I'm looking for a house called Saulsby,' Alice said.

'Saulsby? I don't think...' It was almost sinister the way she whispered and looked furtively over her shoulder. She held the broom a foot from the ground and the leaves began to eddy back, covering the swept path once more. 'You don't mean one of the eyesores?' she said in a voice so low that Alice had to strain to catch it.

'The eyesores?'

'Four nasty little slums. If you've been up the road you must have passed them. They've been due for demolition goodness knows how long.'

Why whisper about it? Why keep glancing up at those blind closed windows? In the heavy shadowed silence of the tree-grown drive Alice suddenly felt a little thrill of fear. If only she had waited until tomorrow when Andrew could have come with her.

'No, it isn't one of those,' she said softly. She glanced behind her quickly into the thick bushes and jumped as the woman hissed suddenly:

'Sorry I had to keep my voice down.' She smiled, breaking the tension, and pointed the broom handle aloft. 'You see, the night-duty girls are all asleep.'

Alice almost laughed as she went once more into the street. She must be letting this business get her down. Of course that was the obvious explanation. Why read ridiculous nuances into it?

While she had been inside the gate someone had parked a bicycle beside her car, a red bicycle. A postman would have a red bicycle, she thought. But where was he? As she stood looking at the blank wall, the long row of gates all overhung with chestnut branches, holly and yellow-spotted laurel, a sudden gust of wind caught the bicycle and knocked it over into the gutter. Its wheels spun. She bent to pick it up. He must have heard the crash and the whirr of wheels, for he came running, slamming the gate of The Laurels.

'Thanks very much.' He was very young with yellow hair and a characterless face in which the colour was oddly distributed, for his chin, nose and forehead were chapped and reddish while his lips and cheeks had a sickly pallor. 'You shouldn't have got yourself dirty.' He hoisted his canvas bag on to the handlebars and stood waiting for her to go.

'Tell me,' she said, 'do you deliver letters down here in the mornings, all the letters? Are you the regular postman?'

'Been on here a couple of months. What were you wanting?'

'Have you ever delivered any letters to a Mrs Nesta Drage at a house called Saulsby?'

'Not what you'd call delivered. There's a redirection notice on Saulsby.'

She stared at him. Her heart had begun to beat very fast. At last the name made sense to somebody besides herself.

'What's a redirection notice?'

'It's like when you change your address, see? You fill in a form at the post office and all the post—well, it doesn't go to your old address. It goes to the new one. We do our own sorting and when we get mail for this said person, the one that's filled in the form, we write the new address on the envelope and it goes back in the post. Saves your letters getting lost like.'

'Would you be very kind and tell me where Mrs Drage's letters are going?'

He shook his head. 'Can't do that. That'd be an invasion of privacy.'

The wind had grown suddenly cold. Twilight was coming and with it a light, needle-sharp frost. She shivered. She was seldom angry but now she could feel herself growing edgy with frustration.

'I suppose it didn't occur to you that there isn't a Saulsby in Chelmsford Road, that it doesn't exist?'

'Now, look,' he said, truculent and defensive, 'it's on the notice. I've seen it on her letters, plain as a pikestaff.'

'Where is it, then? Show me.'

'Up there.' He pushed the bicycle up to the grey terrace and Alice followed.

'Sewerby, you see,' she said quietly, and she was glad she had made no more of this small triumph, for he stared aghast at the name plaque and the flush spread across his whole face, dark as a naevus.

'But I've never had no letters for Sewerby.'

'I'm not surprised. He's a very old man and he's all on his own. I don't suppose anyone ever writes to him, and if you've on here two months—'

He interrupted her raggedly. 'I don't know what come over me.' His voice was pleading and he turned towards her as if he would clutch at her clothes. She moved away, lifting her hand. 'I reckon I must have

misread that name and what with them always coming and going at Kirkby and them houses not having
numbers like…Mr Robson did say I was to check,
but—I don't know—things kind of got on top of me.'
His hands tightened on the handlebars. 'He'll have
the hide off me,' he said.

'I don't want to make trouble for you. I only want to
know where my letters are going.'

'That's easy,' he said eagerly. 'There was a letter
come for her Wednesday.' Alice nodded. She had
posted it herself on Tuesday night. 'One hundred and
ninety-three, Dorcas Street, Paddington. I've got it by
heart on account of my mother's name being Dorcas.'

Alice wrote it down. 'I won't say a word to Mr Robson,' she joked feebly. 'He's not an easy man to see.'

One hundred and ninety-three, Dorcas Street,
Paddington. Of Paddington Alice knew only the station and that small pretty corner known as Little Ven-
ice. Those streets she had seen from Western Region
trains taking her on holiday to Cornwall had been far
from prepossessing. Could Dorcas Street be one of
them? It sounded charming but its very euphony
made her uneasy. In present-day civilisation the
pretty names belonged to sordid venues while a street
that was called The Boltons or Smith Square was all
that was respectable and affluent.

This, then, was the most likely explanation: Nesta
had gone to an ugly slummy part of London but she
had been unable to bring herself to admit it. Snob-
bery, a desire to seem grand to her friends, had made
her give Alice a fine-sounding address.

Her heart contracted with pity as she gave
Chelmsford Road a last look. Nesta must have been to

47

Orphingham and seen in its peace the sanctuary she longed for. Chelmsford Road was the very place she might have chosen for her home if circumstances had been different. Perhaps that too was the explanation of her languor and her depression. A daydreamer continually baulked could have conceived such a plan. Only a woman with a deranged mind would have carried it out. Or—or a woman who lived puzzles, jigsaws, problems on television quiz programmes, the easier crosswords in the evening papers?

Suddenly Alice felt quite excited. Then doubt and disquiet returned. There could be nothing amusing in the motives which had prompted Nesta. She must be rescued. Friendship was pointless if it stopped short at material aid. Alice felt in her handbag the shiny blue book whose cheques never bounced. Why, oh why, instead of this constant effort to keep up appearances, hadn't Nesta told her?

'I'D RATHER YOU DIDN'T GO.'

'Why on earth shouldn't I, darling?' She was at the dressing-table, combing her hair when Andrew had come in, already dressed, slightly impatient. As soon as he had heard she meant to go to Paddington he had said he would go with her, but she had protested. Nesta was proud. She might tolerate Alice enquiring into her affairs, never Andrew.

'Do as you like, but it'll upset you, Bell, if you find she's living with a man.'

'*Nesta?*'

He came towards her and in the mirror she watched him approach and put his hands on her shoulders. 'You're such a child in some ways. I don't mean you're immature and God knows you're always exaggerating your age, but you're innocent. I wonder what you'd do if you found her in some horrible back room with a man—say, Nesta trailing about in a black négligée and the lover not bothering to hide himself, but bellowing things from the bedroom?'

'That's not funny, Andrew.'

'Darling, forgive me, but wouldn't you just whip out the little cheque-book—money, the universal healer?'

She was hurt and she showed it.

'You mean I'm mercenary? I make a god of money?'

'Not a god—a key to open all doors. Bell, I have to tell you this, but that's the way a child feels. Jackie brought Mark and Christopher in tonight—' Diverted, she held the comb poised. She was suddenly appalled because she had forgotten all about them. 'It's all right. I gave them some sweets I found in a drawer. Mark didn't want to go home. D'you know what he said? Let's stay, Mummy. I'll give you sixpence if you'll let me stay.'

'And I'm like that?'

'You're—you're an angel.' He dropped a kiss on to the top of her head. Still troubled, she looked up and in the glass he met her eyes.

Now, as she lifted the heavy mass of hair in both hands and, seeking some way of doing it more flatteringly, held it loosely above her head, he drew back, not touching her any more.

'What's the matter?'

'Don't do your hair like that. I don't like it.' He sounded ridiculously annoyed.

'I thought it made me look younger.'

'For heaven's sake, Bell, don't keep harping on your age as if you were a candidate for a geriatric ward!'

'Sorry.' Still twisting her hair into a soft loose coil, she averted her head from the glass and turned to face him. To her surprise he let out his breath in a sigh.

'It's not so bad, I suppose. I imagine I could get used to it.'

'You won't have to. The old way's easiest.' Rapidly she began weaving the two plaits. 'Look, darling, will you feel better if I promise you that when I find Nesta I'll try to help her without actually giving her money?'

'What other help could you give her?' He was still shaken and she wondered why.

'If she was in need I could bring her here.'

'Bring her *here*? I'd rather you gave her money to stay away, than adopted her!'

'Andrew! Adopt—why did you use that word? What did you mean?'

He shook his head. 'Nothing. Forget it.'

Her hands travelled down over her useless, ageing body. Jackie had been there, Jackie with her two sons. It was not hard to unravel the workings of his subconscious.

'I'm ready now,' she said in a carefully neutral voice. 'Let's go down.'

'GOOD HEAVENS,' SAID UNCLE JUSTIN, 'IT MAKES you wonder what the Post Office is coming to! If you had an idea of your duty as a citizen, Alice, you'd report the whole thing to that fellow—what's-his-name?—Robson.' Suspiciously he ran his tongue round the rim of his glass. 'Where did you get this sherry, Andrew? I may be wrong but to me it has a distinct flavour of the Southern Hemisphere.'

'Well, it can't have,' said Alice firmly. She had recovered her poise, 'since, it came from Jerez. What do *you* think I ought to do about Nesta?'

'Ah, yes, Mrs Drage.' Alice remembered with exasperation that he had to know someone for at least twenty years before venturing on the Christian name. 'A comely woman, very easy to look at. Not at all the sort of person one would expect to see keeping a shop. I daresay she found it difficult to make ends meet.'

'She borrowed some money off Alice once,' said Andrew. Why had she ever told him that? 'Before we were married. I'm afraid there might be a repetition and that's one reason why I think it's better for Alice not to see her.'

'She paid it back,' Alice said pleadingly, 'besides it wasn't much.'

'A couple of hundred pounds and you call it not much!'

51

'Not enough to make a song and dance about,' said Uncle Justin unexpectedly. 'I'm happy to say I was able to give her a little help myself occasionally in that direction.'

Dumfounded, Alice looked at him. He was sitting stiffly, not resting his head against the soft back of the chair. His thinness and the straight set of his shoulders took ten years from his age. His hair was grey but abundant. The bone formation of his face and the sparse flesh had suffered few of the effects of time. There were lines and cavities, deep pouches under the eyes, but there were no wrinkles.

Of all the big men in Salstead he was the biggest. Just as she was wondering if she dare ask him the obvious question Andrew asked it for her. 'And may one ask if you ever got it back?'

His answer would make all the difference. As she waited, half terrified, half curious, for the outburst, the door opened and Pernille appeared on the threshold, beaming at them.

'Ah, dinner!' said Uncle Justin. 'I hope you're going to give us some of your Scandinavian delicacies. I'm particularly fond of those little cup things with asparagus.'

'*Krustader*, Mr Whittaker.'

'That's it. Crustarther. You'll have to give Mrs Johnson the receipt for those.'

Too far away from him to warn him off further indiscreet questioning with a touch, Alice gave Andrew a glance of loving anger.

But he said no more and now her uncle was beaming in happy anticipation of the meal. She felt a sudden impatience, a wish to get the evening over quickly, the night that must pass before she could go to a hundred and ninety-three Dorcas Street, Paddington.

ffffffffffffffff **5** fffff

A KALEIDOSCOPE OF GREEN, GREY AND ROSE-PINK whirled and rocked; then it began to spin round an intensely bright, burning vortex. But just as she thought it must engulf her and destroy the last remaining steadiness of balance the colours split and settled back into the bathroom décor. Just grey tiles, a rectangle of green soap and three pink towels hanging on a wickedly bright rail. The window was like a square of gingham, white bars crossing the black sky of early morning. It was still now, no longer bouncing or swimming in a mist. But the sickness remained. Alice sat down on the edge of the bath. She could not remember ever having felt so ill.

It must be very early. The cold she felt could have nothing to do with the true temperature, for she had turned on the heater when she had first staggered here from the bedroom. Shivers fluttered along her arms and legs and seemed only to increase when she put her hands on the hot rail. In Andrew's shaving glass her face looked white and aged by the bile that was moving again, rising horribly into her mouth. She twisted over to the basin and retched.

Presently, when the spasm had passed, leaving her drained and trembling, she made her way back to the bedroom. Andrew was asleep. The dark blue light that precedes a winter dawn showed her a boy's cheek and a hand curled like a child's round the pillow edge. She moved in beside him warily, afraid to let him see her in the ignominy of a repulsive illness.

But she was *never* ill. Something in Pernille's dinner must have disagreed with her, the pink *silde salat* perhaps, or the *krustader*. Andrew had opened a bottle of wine, *Entre Deux Mers*, a dry white Bourdeaux, but she had taken less than a glassful. And afterwards they had eaten chocolates that Uncle Justin had brought. She shifted away from Andrew, keeping her head up. The very thought of food was bringing the sickness back and the shivers that made her teeth chatter.

She pressed her hands against her diaphragm, willing the nausea to go. Perhaps it had been the yoghurt she had grown so fond of lately and took every night for her supper. As she remembered the gelatinous curd, white, decomposing into whey as the spoon broke it, she threw back the bedclothes and rushed across the room. Let me make it to the bathroom, she prayed.

Of course it had awakened him. She clung to the basin rim, knowing that he was standing behind her.

'Go back to bed,' she said harshly, 'I don't want you to see—'

'Don't be silly.' She knew she would have been sick again if anyone had touched her and yet because he did not touch her she felt, in the midst of her misery, the deprivation.

'I'll be all right in a minute.'

'Why didn't you wake me, Bell? How long have you been like this?'

She ran cold water into the basin, splashed her hands and face. 'Hours,' she said. 'I don't know.'

'Come on.' He put his arms around her and she turned her face away. 'I'll get Pernille to bring you some tea.'

'Leave me alone, please, Andrew.' She fell on to the bed and buried her head in the warm hollow where his had been. 'You mustn't see me like this.'

'Darling, don't be absurd. Aren't you supposed to be the flesh of my flesh and the bone of my bone?' It was a phrase from one of his favourite Victorian novels, half joke, half sincere. 'I'll get Pernille.'

She couldn't drink the tea. It grew cold and bitterly yellow on the bedside table beside the dregs of hot milk Andrew had brought her the night before.

'Pernille,' she said feebly, 'that yoghurt, where did it come from?'

The Danish girl shook out the pillows and pummelled them. 'I took it home from Mr Feast's, Mrs Fielding.'

Alice felt too ill to do her duty and correct the usage. She would never appreciate the difference between 'to bring' and 'to take'.

'Did you have any of it?'

'I? No, thank you. Nobody takes yoghurt but you.'

Andrew came back softly, bringing the morning

papers. She wished he would leave her to the dimness and not snap on the overhead light.

'Any better, darling?'

'I feel terribly ill, Andrew. Do you think we could get Harry?'

'Just because you feel a bit sick?' He sat on the edge of the bed and lifted the long fair hair from her cheeks. 'You'll be better in a little while.'

'And I was going to London today,' she wailed.

'In that case you'd better have Harry. I'm sure he won't let you go out, darling. It's bitterly cold.' To emphasise his words he drew back the curtain and showed the cruel windy morning, clouds white as piled snow, lurching across purplish-black cumulus. The wind was tossing scotch pine branches against the glass, fist-shaped bunches of needles tapping and jerking away again.

'He needn't come till he's finished his other calls.'

His quick jealousy was a better tonic than any medicine Harry could prescribe. 'Don't worry,' he said sharply. 'He'll come.' Catching her eye, he laughed at himself and added ruefully: 'You know very well, darling, if the whole of Salstead was down with bubonic he'd still be here first thing.'

'Andrew!' He must love her, looking not with the eyes but with the mind. 'Go and have your breakfast.' He kissed her, picked up the book he had been reading the night before, and went downstairs.

Harry came as soon as his morning surgery was over. She blushed a little when he came in. Andrew's prophecy had been fulfilled. Bubonic was an exaggeration, but surely Harry had countless patients awaiting him. Andrew must be sitting in the dining-room now, smiling a little, the man in possession. It gave her a little warm thrill to think that, though apart, they shared the same thoughts.

'How do you feel, Alice?'

'Not quite so bad now.' She gave him her hand and he put his fingers to the pulse. 'I was terribly sick earlier. Did Andrew tell you about it?'

His face was expressionless. 'He said something about it on the phone. I didn't disturb him when I came in.' Taking his hand away, he said in a repressed tone, 'He was reading.'

You make him sound like Nero, she thought resentfully, fiddling while Rome burns. Andrew's jealousy was reasonable, the natural corollary to a husband's love, Harry's pathetic.

'I just kept being sick, on and on. I suppose Pernille's dinner was too rich.'

He smiled in disbelief and put the thermometer in her mouth.

'It's more likely to be one of these viruses.'

When she was beginning to think she would vomit again if the glass tube remained any longer between her lips, he took it from her and went to the window.

'It isn't anything serious, is it, Harry? I wanted to go to London today, to Paddington.'

He shook the thermometer down with a swift jerky movement.

'Paddington? You're not going away, are you?'

Strange how to everyone Paddington meant only the station. She shook her head.

'You mustn't think of going out,' he said. 'You'd far better stay where you are. I'll look in again tomorrow.'

Illness was unfamiliar. It made her at once into a

hypochondriac. 'You'd tell me if it was anything serious?' But she knew he wouldn't. Doctors never did.

'I told you, Alice. You've probably got a virus infection. I thought you were looking pale yesterday.'

'Is that why you said I was to come to you if anything was troubling me?'

He blushed as hotly as the young postman in the twilit street. 'Of course,' he said abruptly. At the best of times he had no poise, only a vulnerable boyish gaucheness. Now as, all thumbs, he bundled his instruments back into the case, she thought briefly back over the ten years since he had come to Salstead. She had lost count of how many times he had asked her to marry him. And yet for all that, their relationship had never advanced beyond friendship, he had never kissed her or even put his arm round her shoulders. They were doctor and patient. She almost smiled as she thought that in spite of the love and the proposals the question of ending *that* relationship had never arisen. Her physical health had been so splendid she had never had to call him in.

'I hope I'm not going to be ill long,' she said fretfully. It was going to be awkward and embarrassing if he had to come here daily to attend her.

'Here's someone to cheer you up,' he said.

It was Hugo. Muffled in a rugger scarf, he tiptoed up to the bed and dumped a squashy parcel on his sister's stomach. 'Grapes,' he said. 'Hallo, Harry.'

'How did you know I was ill?'

'News travels fast in this neck of the woods. Jackie bumped into Pernille Madsen at the shops.' He rubbed his hands and sat down heavily on the bed. 'You're in the best place. It's enough to freeze the—'

'All right, Hugo!' Alice laughed weakly. 'Good-bye, Harry. It was nice of you to come.' He hesitated, waiting—for what? What did he expect her to say to him, what could she say that was kind, generous and meaningless all at the same time? 'You mustn't think that because I'm a friend...' As the smile on his face gradually chilled, she blundered on, 'I mean, you mustn't neglect your other patients for me....'

His hand was resting on the glass fingerplate of the door. Then she saw that it was no longer resting, but pressing, pressing, until the nails showed white.

'What makes you think you're different from anyone else, Alice?' he snapped. Hugo coughed and, making a great display of loosening his scarf, flung it on the bed. 'Are you criticising my professional conduct?'

She was horrified, almost at a loss for words. 'I didn't... I wouldn't... You know what I meant!'

'I'm sorry. Forget it.' He cleared his throat and managed a smile. 'I'll leave a prescription with Miss Madsen,' he said abruptly. 'Take care of yourself.' Then he was gone.

'What was all that about?' Hugo asked.

'I don't know.'

'He's very fond of you, you can see that. It's written all over him.'

'Never mind that,' said his sister impatiently. 'Oh, Hugo, I did so want to go up to London today. D'you think...'

'No, I don't. You'll get pneumonia.'

'You wouldn't go for me, would you?'

'Not on your life. We've got people coming to lunch. Why d'you want to go there, anyway?'

She told him about the postman and the redirection notice, and he laughed in grudging admiration of Nesta's cunning.

'Good psychology, that. Women always read such a hell of a lot into an address. I know Jackie always wants to pick our holiday hotels by their names, and when you get there the Miramar turns out to be a slum on top of the marshalling yards.'

'But Saulsby wasn't there at all.'

'I can't see why she bothered to write. Why not just vanish?'

Yes, why not? The second letter was explained by the receipt of the parcel. But why had Nesta written the first letter suddenly, out of the blue? She couldn't have known Alice had the ring, for she hadn't mentioned it then. It was uncanny that she should have been silent for a month and then have written just as Alice was going to advertise for her. It was, at any rate, a remarkable coincidence.

'I didn't keep either of the letters, but I remember what they said. The first one said something like this: *Dear Alice, just a line to let you know I'm settled in temporarily, but I shan't be staying for very long. I don't suppose we shall meet again, but thanks for the meal and everything. Best wishes to Andrew and your uncle.*'

'Just an ordinary sort of letter,' said Hugo. Alice sighed, knowing from experience that his own were very much like that. 'It told you the basic essentials.'

'It told me nothing,' said Alice unhappily. 'The second one was even worse. *Thanks for the ring. I enclose two pounds to cover cost....* And, Hugo, that was another odd thing. I've only just thought of it. I'd paid Cropper's but I didn't say what it had cost and I didn't ask for the money. But the bill was for two pounds and Nesta sent me exactly two pounds.'

'Coincidence?'

'Well, it *must* have been. Then she wrote: *Don't put yourself out to answer this as I've never been much of a correspondent*, and then something about being too pre-occupied to bother. Not as rude as I've made it sound of course. She ended up with the usual sort of regards to Andrew and Uncle Justin.'

'Keen on him, wasn't she?'

Something seemed to grip her chest, something which released a cold bubble of nausea.

'What *do* you mean?'

'Justin.'

'Oh.' She was able to smile again. 'What makes you think so?'

'She used to make him up a buttonhole every morning.'

'You're romancing, Hugo. Those flowers came from the garden.'

'Did they hell! Not for the last two years they didn't. Your little Nesta had an eye for the men.' He smiled and in the smile was a kind of wry vanity. 'She made a pass at me once,' he said thoughtfully.

'She did what?'

'Come off it, Alice. You know what a pass is as well as I do.' He glanced at her doubtfully. 'Almost as well, anyway. She'd been baby-sitting for us and I drove her home. She said would I see her into the shop because she was nervous in the dark. You know how slow and languid she was. There wasn't much in it but she sort of swayed against me in the dark. I put out my arm to stop her falling and she—well, she took hold of me and said she was so miserable, I mustn't leave her alone. I yanked her upstairs, put all the lights on and got out double-quick.'

As Alice stared at him he went on hurriedly: 'The funny thing was after that, whenever we were alone together—you know, if we met in the street just for a moment—she'd talk to me—Oh, damn it! It's so hard to explain. She'd talk to me as if we'd had a full-blown affair and had to kind of—well, keep it secret. She kept saying Jackie mustn't ever know. But there wasn't anything *to* know. I don't mind telling you, just between ourselves, I used to wonder what she would say if she ever got to be alone with Jackie and she was manic as against depressive.'

Alice was rather shocked. 'Manic-depressive? You mean she was really ill in her mind? Oh, Hugo, I think it was just loneliness and perhaps envy.' He shrugged, disbelieving. 'I don't think we any of us realized how lonely she was.' She looked up at him, wondering how he would take sentimentality. 'She told me once losing her husband had been like losing a leg or an arm. Part of her was in the grave with him.'

'She was a mistress of the cliché.' The door had swung open and Andrew was on the threshold, holding the coffee tray. Alice sat up, startled by his silent, almost supernatural arrival.

'Oh, darling! I remember she said—'

'And I remember,' he interrupted her, 'how she used to call a sheaf a sheath and a corsage a cortège.' As Hugo chuckled he moved towards the bed and took her face gently in his hands. 'You're better, Bell. You've got some colour in your cheeks.'

With a word, a smile, he could make her feel like a beauty. Feeling warmth coming back to flush her face, she put up her hands to the things she was proud of, the white, still unlined neck and the long loose hair.

'I think I could drink some coffee,' she said.

'I've brought you another visitor.'

He brushed his lips against her forehead in a fluttering kiss. Embarrassed, Hugo shifted uneasily.

'What's supposed to be the matter with you?' asked Uncle Justin from the doorway. He was frowning. Alice noticed the chrysanthemum bud in his buttonhole and remembered the roses, wound and wired in silver foil, he had worn in the summer.

'I'm supposed to have a virus.'

'A virus! I don't know what we're all doing in here, then. That's a fine thing to spread about the works.' With extreme ostentation, he shook out a large white handkerchief and held it yashmak-wise across his nose and mouth. 'I suppose a virus is a new-fangled name for the flu?'

'I'll get up when I've had my coffee,' she said meekly, knowing he would discourage malingering.

His reply surprised her. 'I wouldn't.' He sat on the dressing-table stool as far away from the bed as possible. 'You've got Andrew here and what's-her-name to wait on you.' Pausing, he added characteristically: 'It isn't as if you've got anything to do.'

Perhaps it would be better to stay where she was. Certainly everyone was very anxious that she should stay in bed. The coffee tasted strong and bitter. Over the rim of the cup she watched them all in silence.

Harry hadn't actually said it was a virus, just that it probably was. He hadn't said that she had a raised temperature either. It was true what Uncle Justin said about a virus just being the flu, but she had never had flu before. Surely there would be more to it than these waves of sickness that came so chillingly and overmasteringly, but when they had gone, left her feeling well and even cheerful?

As she sipped the coffee a strange thought visited her. That was how Nesta had been, alternating between illness and health, only Nesta's had been not of the body but of the mind. Nesta had been manic-depressive, Hugo said. Why had she, Alice, she who was never ill, suddenly developed this strange illness, when she was on the point of finding Nesta?

The malaise returned sharply, washing over her, and drawing the blood from her face. She felt the pallor and the chill which came with it and her whole body jerked in a big convulsive shudder.

Hugo and her uncle were discussing some change at the works. Only Andrew noticed. He took her hand and held it until the spasm had passed. She leant back against the pillows, spent, and inexplicably afraid.

6

On Monday morning, as soon as Andrew had gone, she got up. After two days in bed she still felt tired, but in her weariness there was no desire for sleep, only a weakness that seemed to come from some inner core of her body. The sickness had passed, leaving her languid and strangely prone to tears. She had no appetite except for liquids, but even tea and the yoghurt she had lately grown so fond of tasted odd, bitter yet otherwise flavourless. The fluid seemed to burn her throat.

But there was nothing really wrong with her. Harry had come again on Sunday and shrugged off her fears. It was just a mild virus, he thought, not absolutely committing himself. His words were reassuring, but she hadn't liked the look in his eyes. There was bewilderment in them, doubt and concern.

The fresh air would do her good. It was a pity the wind was so strong, stirring the bare black branches of the Vair shrubs so that their tops looked like a dark and stormy sea, but it couldn't be helped. She would wrap up warm and wear a scarf on her head. Besides it was always warmer and more sheltered in London than in the country.

The thought that in less than two hours' time she would see Nesta again provided her with a little spurt of energy. The house in Dorcas Street might be a bit of a shock. Of course Nesta didn't own it, nor even have a flat in it, but a single poor little back room. She, Alice, would make a stoical effort not to show her dismay. If Nesta were out of work—as she probably would be, a very minor assistant in a huge West End shop—she would just ask the landlady where the shop was and make her way there. She would take Nesta out to lunch. Dizzily she thought of taxis, of the Savoy, of wine brought by a deferential waiter.

'When I've gone,' she said to Pernille, 'you can ring up Dr. Blunden and tell him I'm so much better he needn't bother to call.'

'I am not good with the telephone, Mrs. Fielding.' The Danish girl had brown skin, darker than her hair, and eyes as blue and pleading as a Siamese kitten's.

'Then you obviously need practice,' said Alice firmly. 'I'll tell you what, when I'm out I'll get you a five-shilling stamp and a half-crown one for your brother. Is he still collecting?'

Pernille's willing-to-please smile quirked up even further at the corners and she broke into a giggle. 'Oh, yes, Knud is a famous...' The word came out on a bubble of proud laughter, '...philatelist!'

'I won't forget.'

Nesta ought to have a present, too. Alice wondered

why she hadn't thought of it before. It was unlike her to go and visit someone empty-handed. She felt ashamed of herself, almost thankful that she hadn't found Nesta in Orphingham. To arrive without a gift when Nesta was probably in need.... She was appalled and puzzled at her own thoughtlessness.

Alice sincerely believed that she knew London. You must know a city if all your life you had lived only twenty-five miles from it. In fact she knew it less well than certain holiday resorts. The City itself she had seen only from car windows, its buildings like a series of photographs in a guide book that has been quickly flipped through. She was well acquainted with a few square yards of pavement outside most of the theatres and could easily visualise the river between the Tower and Westminister Bridge. At the age of ten she had been able to name all the bridges in their correct sequence just as she could count up to twenty in French. In fact she knew her capital as well as most Englishwomen know it; all her knowledge was of the two or three streets in which she had bought clothes.

From Liverpool Street she took the Tube and she remembered how often she had made just this same journey with Nesta. They had always got out at Marble Arch and walked back, window-gazing. Nesta's tastes had been expensive—the black she always wore had to cost a lot if it was to look nice—and sometimes Alice had slipped her a couple of pounds when the salesgirl wasn't looking. It seemed cruel not to be able to have the sombre dresses you only wore out of respect for your dead husband's memory. Alice had bought nothing for herself, but only followed where Nesta led.

Today she had no guide. Still, it was easy to buy
presents for someone as pretty and vain as Nesta,
floral scent, a scarf of white silk scribbled all over
with black. Alice came out of the shop and hailed a
taxi. It was only the second time in her life she had
ever done such a thing in London. The driver ac-
cepted her directions, questioned nothing. She felt
brave and rather sophisticated. London was just a
place like any other, Salstead or Orphingham magni-
fied.

Once past Marble Arch again, she was lost. They
might be anywhere, in any great city. She leaned
back and closed her eyes. The tiredness was coming
back and with it a physical unease that was too faint
to amount to sickness or even the warning of sickness
to come. It was just discomfort and nervous anticipation. She sat up and looked out of the window.

They were nearly there. As they turned out of big
busy thoroughfare she caught sight of a name on a
house wall, Dorcas Street. This, at last, was where
Nesta lived.

It was neither sordid nor romantic, and it was not a
slum. The houses were very tall and ranged in long
plaster-covered terraces, each with a pillared portico
and little iron-railed balconies. They had a shabby,
neglected look. The roadway, treeless and uniformly
grey, seemed like a reflection of the wind-stirred grey
sky, itself an avenue between long architraves.

She couldn't see much of a hundred and ninety-
three. Stopping directly outside it, the taxi's bulk hid
everything but its two fat pillars and its flight of steps.
At home Alice would hardly have thought twice about
how much to tip Mr Snow. Now she was a little flus-

tered. A ten-shilling note? It seemed all right, enough, at any rate, to evoke a large pleased smile. It was only after he had turned that it occurred to her she might have asked him to wait. Her new-found courage was unequal to calling after him.

She sighed and went to the steps. Where the number should have been on the column that supported the canopy was only a blank rectangle, a paler patch on the plaster. Slowly she lifted her head and let her gaze travel upwards. There on the pediment, scrawled in neon tubing was a frail attempt at smartness, were the words *Endymion Hotel*.

IT WAS HAPPENING ALL OVER AGAIN. FOR A BRIEF wild moment her brain registered a mad picture of another redirection notice, indeed a whole series of them, directing her from one house to another back and forth the length and breadth of the country. No, that was impossible, just stupid panicky guesswork.

She stood under the canopy, looking up at the name, at the plaster patch where the number should have been, and suddenly as she waited, half afraid to take that first look through the glass, a violent spasm of nausea washed over her so that she swayed against the wall. It passed with slow cruelty, leaving her legs cramped and stiff.

She took a deep breath of not very fresh air and pushed the door open.

Because she had expected squalor her first sight of the foyer came as a pleasant surprise. It had been recently modernised. The Victorian panelled doors had been faced with hardboard, the moulded ceiling boxed in with polystyrene tiles and a new floor laid of black and white blocks. At ceiling level she could see a curly plaster leaf, part perhaps of a Corinthian capital, peeping between strips of plastic. Gladioli and roses, made out of wafer-thin wax, stuck out like a sunburst from a simulated marble urn. Behind the acid-yellow counter sat a young man on a high stool writing something in a book.

The doors had made no noise and for a moment he didn't see her. She stood by the flowers—seen close-to, they were grimed with dust which had settled into and become part of their petals and calyxes—and as she hesitated somebody opened a door at the back of the hall.

It swung back as if of its own accord and through it she caught a dillusioning glimpse of what the rest of the place must be like. She saw a passage, its wall, faced with ochre-coloured lincrista, its floor covered by threadbare haircord torn on the threshold into a frayed hole. Then someone pushed the door suddenly, a woman who heaved her back against it and whose hair was a bright gauzy blonde.

Sickness and shyness were dispelled by excitement. Alice went up to the counter.

'Can you tell me if Mrs Drage is in?'

'Not what you'd call *in*. She's not a resident.' His complexion had the thick bloodlessness of skin on wet white fish. He wetted his fleshy lips and stared at her with blank boredom, swinging his legs as if to the tempo of some silent but remembered pop tune.

'But you do know her? She has been here?'

He just glanced at her handbag and her expensive gloves, then at the delicate wrappings on Nesta's presents. 'I haven't seen Mrs. Drage for, let's see—three months. Oh, it'd be all of that. It's funny you asking. I wouldn't remember her on account of all...' He grinned ironically and she felt the grin was aimed at her, '...all the thousands we get passed through our doors.' Alice shifted impatiently. 'I say I wouldn't remember her only Mr Drage come in himself about half an hour ago.'

'*Mr* Drage?' Alice clasped the edge of the counter, longing for a chair. Before she could stop herself she burst out, 'But she's a widow, there isn't a Mr Drage!'

He didn't wink. He yawned very slightly and gave a faint shrug. His background was perhaps as different from hers as possible, his outlook as unlike hers as was consistent with their both being human beings and of British nationality. 'Is that so? Yeah, well, live and let live. Maybe she got married again. I'd say it was her business, wouldn't you?'

The telephone rang. He gabbled into it, using a good many yeahs. Alice stood looking at him helplessly. Nesta hadn't been at the Endymion for three months, but her letters had been sent on to her from Orphingham to Endymion.

While he talked she got out her diary and turned back to August. Nesta had left Salstead on August the eighth. She put on her reading glasses and walked away from the counter to stand under the rather dim centre light. *August seventh, Friday, Pernille not well. Harry says mostly mental, probably homesickness. Must do what I can to cheer her up. Perhaps a really nice present? Nesta to supper. Still very hot.*

August eighth, Saturday. Nesta leaving today. Raining hard.

'Did Mrs Drage come here on August eighth?'

He put the receiver down. 'You the police?'

'Do I look like the police?'

Perhaps policewomen dressed like she did when they were in plain clothes. As soon as she had asked the question she wished instead that she had had the courage to sustain the bluff. On the other hand— how much did you tip or bribe people like him?

'If it's her address you want,' he said suddenly, 'I haven't a clue. Mr Drage only come in to collect her mail.'

'Her mail?' Alice's voice sounded hollow and echoing as if someone else had spoken the words.

'Yeah. Well, if that's all I've got things to do.'

The sickness was coming back. Fighting it off, she said rather wildly, 'Please tell me...' It wouldn't do to give him too little. She opened her handbag, and, firmly shutting away thoughts of Andrew's and Uncle Justin's horror, laid a five-pound note on the counter top.

For a moment his face hardly changed. Then the wet red lips melted into a knowing smile.

'What's she done, then?'

'Nothing. I can't find her. I only want to find her.'

'Yeah, well...' The plump little hand had long nails. It closed over the note and thrust it into the pocket of his jacket through which gold thread ran, appearing occasionally like a recurrent vein of ore. He opened the book he had been writing in when Alice arrived.

'August eighth, you said? Mrs Drage booked up for that night but she never come. Mr Drage called up and cancelled it. She never come at all but we got mail for her. Three or four letters it was and a little parcel.'

'And you gave them to this man who came in this morning?'

'I gave them to Mr Drage, yeah. Why not?'

A big man in Salstead.... If he could only give her some clue to the appearance of 'Mr Drage'. He wriggled a little on his stool and began to buff his nails on his jacket lapel.

'You knew him well?' she said tentatively.

'Sure I did. Him and his wife been coming here on weekends God knows how long. From the country it was—some dump in Essex.'

Her heart leapt. This man might well be someone she knew.

'Then you must often have had a close look at him,' she said, forcing a smile and trying to make her voice persuasive. A description, she prayed, make him give me a description. 'You were alone with him this morning. I'm sure you...' She stopped. Suddenly his face had become hideously aggressive and he got slowly and deliberately off his stool. What had she said? Was there some limit to how much the bribe would buy? He leant across the counter and thrust his face into hers.

'What are you getting at?' he said. He was no more than five feet four, small-boned and sinuous as a girl. 'You insinuating something, are you?'

Alice had no idea what he meant, but she sensed something foul and alien. With a little gasp she backed away from him, slipping on the waxed floor. Her hands found the door as if by instinct and she stumbled out into the windy street.

A taxi, she must find a taxi. Clutching Nesta's presents she ran along Dorcas Street until she came to the main road. It was full of office workers hurrying to lunch places. After her encounter with the Endymion receptionist it was a comfort just to be with ordinary people, but how strange, how frightening, to notice how many of them looked like Nesta! Little heels tapped, short skirts lifted by the wind showed plump knees; pretty dolls' faces, their pink mouths snapping as they chattered, were topped by twists and bunches and doughnuts of yellow hair. She realised, but not newly, rather as if subconsciously she had always known it, that this was supposed to be the ideal type of womanhood. The fairness, the silliness, the porcelain skin—these were what attracted the majority of men, what they made jokes about, yet coveted.

She came up to the wider pavement and mingled with the crowd of little blonde ghosts. Ghosts, why had she thought of that? It made her shiver.

The first taxi was taken, the second pulled in beside her as she gave a feeble wave. It had been a disastrous morning and suddenly she knew she couldn't face the Tube.

'Will you take me all the way to Liverpool Street?'

The notes she could feel in her wallet were as comforting as a drug.

'MY POOR BELL,' SAID ANDREW, SMILING. 'I WISH I'd been there. I'd love to have seen you taken for a policewoman.'

'It was horrible.' She began to pull the curtains,

shutting out the garden, the windy night and the dark orange moon that was rising above Vair Place. 'I suppose I shall have to give up looking for her now.'

Andrew pulled the sofa up to the fire and tucked a cushion behind her head. 'You suppose? I thought the mystery was solved.'

'It isn't really. Not all of it. How could she write and thank me for the ring when she hadn't even got it? And why did that man go to the Endymion only this morning to get the letters? It's—well, it's such a fantastic coincidence.'

'It would be, but for one thing.' She looked up at him enquiringly, hoping wistfully for reassurance. He dropped a quick kiss on her cheek. 'You don't know the letters and the parcel were yours at all, do you?'

'But I—Andrew, I didn't actually ask him where they came from. I just assumed—"

"You just assumed. If the place is used as an accommodation address they might have dozens of letters for her. The boy friend could have been coming in once a week to fetch them.'

'That wasn't the impression I got, darling. I'm sure he meant that that was his first visit and that he took *all* the letters.'

A flicker of impatience crossed his face and pulled at the mouth muscles. Then he controlled it and, smiling, looked at her searchingly.

'How can you talk about impressions when you say yourself you weren't feeling well?'

Firelight like candlelight is flattering. She could feel it playing on her face, then realised with a little pang that she had not powdered her nose or painted her lips since the morning. Was that why he was staring at her so closely?

'You were ill and nervous and uneasy,' he said. 'Don't underrate your imagination. Bell.'

'No, you're right. You're always right.' She curled her legs under her and rested her head on his shoulder. The book he had been reading lay face-downwards on the cushions, a book with a chocolate-brown jacket, its title and illustration enclosed in rectangles of greenish blue. She watched his hand creep across to it. There was something loving and hungry and at the same time surreptitious in the way he slid it on to his lap.

'Go on,' she laughed, 'you can read it if you like. I won't disturb you.'

Compulsive reading was just escapism. Why should he want to escape, and what was he escaping from? He was tired, she thought, it was only natural.

The fireplace wall was lined with bookshelves. The Trollope clericals and politicals had pride of place at eye level on the third shelf from the top. All the politicals had that same blue and brown cover. She smiled to herself as she realised that she had never yet seen the complete set there on the shelves. At least one was always out, actually in Andrew's hands, on the table or by their bed.

She looked at him covertly but he was already too preoccupied to notice the movement of her eyes. Wasn't it rather odd for a man to keep reading the same novels over and over again? He must know them by heart. She wondered vaguely how important to him was the world they presented. By now it must be very real to him, part of his daily consciousness, a

source of metaphor, a guide to speech. Amid these
reflections came a sudden conviction that to be a true
companion to him she ought also to be acquainted
with that world. It was what people meant when they
talked about 'having things in common.' You needn't
as much of that as you could get when you had
disadvantages that couldn't be overcome—the difference in age, for instance, the threat of child-
lessness. . . .

She got up. He turned a page and smiled at some
favourite expression that had caught his eye. Smiling
like that, uninhibitedly, indifferent to observation as a
child is, he looked terribly young, younger even than
he was. She was suddenly very much aware of her
thirty-eight years.

The dining-room door was ajar. As she crossed the
hall she peered through the dark room towards the
uncurtained french windows that showed the shrubbery and the side of Vair Place. It was unpleasant to
think that she had sat on that lawn, under those
trees, a big strong child nearly five feet tall and already reading quite grown-up books, when Andrew
had not even been born.

She went upstairs into her bedroom and switched
on the light over the dressing-table glass. Then she
felt in the drawer for the only lipstick she possessed.

Slowly she lifted her head and her eyes met her
own reflection. There was not much light in the room
and the furniture behind her lay in shadow. Apart
from her own face the mirror showed only vague
shapes and the pale shimmer of flowers in a vase.

Her hair was very untidy, coming loose in front
from its braids and irradiated into translucent gold by

the overhead light. Puzzled, very slightly alarmed, she drew back and closed her eyes. After an interval she opened them again. The impression was still there. Her own face looked unfamiliar and at the same time familiar. It seemed fuller, blanker, drained of intelligence. In some ways it looked younger for the skin was clear and glowing and the eyes bright.

'Pull yourself together,' she said aloud, but the brisk, hackneyed phrase which she could see as well as heard herself speak only enhanced the—the what? Hallucination?

Quickly she combed back her hair. As she painted two lines of strawberry red on her mouth the illusion vanished. With a sigh of relief she straightened up. She was herself again.

ffffffffffffffffff 7 ffffff

A WICKED WIND FROM THE NORTH-EAST WHIS-
tled down the twin-track road and howled away
under the concrete bridge. At the entrance to the by-
pass the oil-drums had been taken away and in their
place someone had stretched a long white ribbon of
the kind seen on wedding cars.

In spite of the cold a crowd had gathered to watch
the official opening: children from the primary
school, shepherded by a harassed teacher; shop assis-
tants out for their lunchtime break; housewives with
baskets. Behind the ribbon stood the Parliamentary
Secretary to the Ministry of Transport, surprisingly
feminine as if it were not surprise enough that she
was female; Justin Whittaker who was chairman of
the highways committee; the chairman of the council; and a host of hangers-on who had nothing to do
but watch, applaud and ultimately eat smoked

salmon and roast chicken with the great ones at The
Boadicea.

'There can scarcely be an inhabitant of Salstead,'
Justin Whittaker was saying, 'who will not regard the
opening of this by-pass as an unmixed blessing. I
think I speak for all of us when I say that it is with
disquiet and apprehension that we have watched the
daily shaking—nay, undermining—of our historic
buildings by the constant passage...'

Andrew squeezed Alice's arm. 'Oh, adjourn, adjourn!' he yawned.

'Sssh!'

'Nor will it deprive us of the trade necessary to our
continued prosperity, for the slip road which leaves it
and meets the town centre will allow access to those
vehicles whose entry is a commercial necessity. This
slip road is a triumph of contemporary engineering.
Not only is it a most modern highway of its kind, but
its designers have seen to it that Helicon Lane, to
which it runs parallel, remains untouched to con-
tinue as a beauty spot of which we may all be justly
proud.'

An icy drizzle had begun to fall. He raised the collar of his barathea overcoat and stepping back,
handed a pair of shears to the Parliamentary Secretary. She drew her furs more closely around her and,
still clasping the violets presented to her by one of the
schoolchildren, cut the ribbon.

'I declare the Salstead By-pass well and truly open.'
She had a voice like the Queen's, high-pitched,
poised, remote.

Andrew nudged Alice. 'And may God save her and

all who drive on her,' he said. She laughed and held his arm more tightly, flinching from the bitter, rain-bearing wind.

The Parliamentary Secretary scuttled back to her car in thin court shoes. Her driver stood holding the door open. Presently the car moved off along the virgin track, followed by Justin Whittaker's Bentley, the chairman's Rolls and so on down to the Mini that belonged to the assistant sanitary inspector. The Parliamentary Secretary waved graciously, again like a royal lady in a state procession.

'Come along, children,' said the schoolmistress. 'I'd like the first dinner people in the vanguard, please.'

'Are you going to the luncheon?' Alice asked Harry Blunden.

'I'm not a local dignitary. G.P.s are hoi-polloi these days.'

'We've got a double ticket,' Alice said. 'Nepotism, really, because I'm a Whittaker, but Andrew's got to get back to the works.' She realized suddenly what she had said and what he might expect. There was no reason why he shouldn't come with her in Andrew's place. Walking between the two men, she glanced quickly from the smooth handsome head to the tousled one. Then Andrew's hand holding hers pressed very gently, relaxing again at once. It was an indication that he wouldn't care for the substitution. 'Of course I shan't go,' she said too emphatically.

'And you're better now, Alice?' Again that odd, solicitous look. 'Miss Madsen rang me yesterday and said you were better.'

'Nearly back to normal.'

'I'll look in again in a day or two, shall I?'

Andrew was holding the Sprite door open for her.

'Really, I don't think that's necessary,' he said smoothly. Harry blushed, screwing up his face against the squally wind. 'We can always contact you if...' He paused and said emphatically, '...if my wife needs another prescription.' The speed with which he hustled her into the car was almost rough. 'We may as well take advantage of the triumph of the contemporary engineering,' he said.

The slip road left the by-pass smoothly and gradually at a narrow acute angle. Inside this angle the end of Helicon Lane could be seen, cut off by the great embankments of still grassless earth. They were like raw edges of a wound made in the fields.

Reflecting that she had not been down Helicon Lane since Nesta's departure, Alice leaned over and looked down. The branches of the Salstead Oak seemed to sweep the sky like the bristles of a huge brush. She could just see The Bridal Wreath, its twin bow windows now filled with skeins of wool and canvases printed for gros point. The sign had been replaced by another, The Workbasket. She sighed, losing sight of it in the mist her breath had made on the glass.

The road passed between stretches of barren earth. A fence had been put up almost against the nave of St. Jude's Church and nothing remained of the old churchyard. It was rather awe-inspiring to think that the new concrete over which they were driving covered what had once been consecrated ground. Here had been green mounds, moss-grown slabs and between them long yew-shaded avenues. Mourners had walked there, country people in smocks and print gowns, bringing stocks and nasturtiums from cottage gardens. Alice shook herself and said prosaically:

'I can't very well go to the luncheon now.'

'For heaven's sake, darling!'

'How can I, after what I said to Harry?' And after what you said, she thought.

'You can change your mind at the last moment,' he said jesuitically. 'Pernille won't have anything for you at home.' He glanced into the wing mirror. 'I'd better speed up if we don't want to get involved with the motorcade, or whatever it's called.'

Still doubtful, she let him drop her in the High Street. It was full of people, mostly people she knew. What did it matter if they saw him take her in his arms and kiss her full on the mouth? They were still on their honeymoon and it would go on being like this until they were both old, so old that the nine years between them was nothing. She was still radiant from the kiss as she crossed the road and went into The Boadicea.

The lounge was already crowded. A waiter approached her with a tray of glasses and she took one containing something pale yellow with a crescent of lemon peel slotted on to its rim. Through the glass door that led by way of a beamed tunnelly passage to the dining-room she could see tables laid with white cloths, silver, late dahlias in long narrow vases. The door swung and stuck open as a waitress came through. With her drifted a pungent garlicky smell of soup.

Alice put down her glass abruptly, suddenly and sharply sickened. The dry martini trickled coldly down her throat meeting a fierce surge of something that made her gasp. It was exactly as if her chest and stomach were being scalded from within. She sagged against a table, avoiding the solicitous eyes of Mrs Graham whose husband kept the hotel.

— How could she dream of eating in company, feeling as she did? Before she was half-way through that soup she would be jerking back her chair, flying for the door with a napkin pressed against her mouth. Far better to go now before people came with their questions and their steadying arms.

She staggered towards the door burrowing between knots of guests. Their laughter and their bright brittle talk stabbed at her with little points of pain. The wind that met her was cruel too, assailing her with mischievous teasing gusts. Just as she gained the shelter of Mr Cropper's shop porch Uncle Justin and the Parliamentary Secretary left their cars. He hadn't seen her. She kept her back turned for a moment, gazing at the swimming masses of rings and brooches, until they had crossed the pavement.

Then she began to walk up the High Street. The cutting wind seemed to beat at her with little slaps. No wonder the ancients had personalised winds, she thought, seeing them as gods or puff-cheeked cherubs, blowing with capricious malice.

It was half a mile to Vair House and Andrew had taken the car with him to the works. The hourly bus service to Pollington which had formerly passed Vair had been diverted from this moment to the by-pass. The obvious person to help her was Harry, but she couldn't go to Harry now. I shall *have* to walk, she told herself fiercely.

She managed another twenty yards or so until her

legs threatened to buckle and yield. Her whole body felt unutterably weak and beaten, empty of everything but urgent fear. She had never been ill in all her life and now when illness had come it was like some huge venomous snake that wrapped her in coils of pain and panic. Gasping, she tottered up to the seat on the war memorial green and sank on to the thick oak board.

There was only one thing to do. She would have to hire a car. When she had had five minutes' rest she could probably just make it to Snow's.

Presently the drumming in her ears stopped and the coils relaxed. It was, she imagined, just like having a bandaged limb unbound, only in this case it wasn't a limb but her entire body. She raised herself gingerly and set off again along the pavement.

'Salstead Cars. Self-drive or chauffeur-driven cars for every occasion.' They had hired her wedding cars from here. From the windows of one of these black limousines she had waved to Mrs Johnson as she and Uncle Justin drove off down the drive of Vair Place.

The office was a creosoted wooden hut around which the great glossy cars clustered like seals. Perched on a high stool, his hat pushed to the back of his head, the proprietor sat eating sandwiches off a copy of the *Daily Mirror.* He got off the stool when she came in.

'Oh, Mr Snow, I'm afraid I'm not very well. I suddenly feel so awfully faint and I wondered...' She tried to smile, averting her face from the slabs of bread and corned beef.

'Here, have a chair, Mrs Fielding.' She dropped heavily into a bentwood chair with a broken cane

seat. 'You're as white as a ghost. Now, if you were to ask me what I would advise is a little drop of brandy.'

'Brandy? Oh, no, I couldn't . . .'

'It's wonderful for settling the stomach.' Ignoring her objections, he fetched a quarter-bottle from the shelf and with it a surprisingly clean glass. 'Warm the cockles of your heart, that will.'

'Thank you. It's very kind of you.'

The effect of the brandy was immediate. Unexpectedly it didn't burn, but flooded her with soft civilising warmth like the newly inhaled scene of fresh flowers. Fountains and sprays, healing and gentle, grew and cascaded all over her body.

Mr Snow wrapped up his sandwiches and stood by the small grimy window, whistling softly through his teeth.

'Don't happen to have heard from Mrs Drage, do you?' he asked suddenly.

'Well . . .'

'I only wondered, you and her being so friendly like. Feeling better now, are you?'

'Much better. Mr Snow, why did you ask about Mrs Drage?'

'Well, it was in the way of business, Mrs Fielding. But I won't worry you now, you being under the weather.'

'Oh, no, really, I'd like to hear.'

'You understand there's no offense meant, Mrs Fielding?' He took the glass, rubbed it with a bit of newspaper and inverted it on the shelf. Firmly she suppressed a shudder. 'Only it's like this, we did a couple of jobs for Mrs D. and seeing as she didn't leave no address . . .'

'You mean she owes you money?'

He opened the booking ledger on top of the desk. 'August seventh it was. Seventh and eighth.' Alice bit her lip, once more uneasy. 'She booked one of my vehicles to take some stuff up to Feasts' for her. Three p.m.' Those were the words Daphne had used—'some stuff', 'she left some stuff at our place!' 'We did the job and she says to come to The Bridal Wreath the next morning. August eighth, eight sharp, she said, and pick her up and take her to the station. She was staying the night at Feasts' but coming back the next morning to see to the removals. We was to take her to the station and stop at Feasts' for the stuff on route. Eight o'clock sharp, she said. I don't mind telling you I was a bit narked. I took the car round myself but she'd gone. Not a word from her. She'd flitted on her own.'

'Are you sure?'

'They were taking out the furniture, Mrs Fielding. Cox's from York Street it was. The doors were all open and I went up. Len Cox was there taking out her bits and pieces. Where is she then? I said, not wanting to hang about on account of Saturday always being busy. Gone, he said. We was here at seven and the key was in the door so we came up. The place was as neat as a pin, Len said, all packed up and ready to go. You can't just take it, I said, not without her here, but Len's very hasty. It was going into store, he said, and she'd paid up when he gave her the estimate. I can't have some bloody woman messing me about, he said —Pardon me, Mrs Fielding, but that's what he said.

'Well, I wasn't laughing, I can tell you. I'd turned down two jobs for eight o'clock and one of them

would have brought in five nicker. Not only that. There was what she owed me for going to Feasts' with the van in the afternoon.'

Alice said quickly, 'Of course I'll make that good, Mr Snow.' She found her cheque-book and began to write, surprised at the firmness of her hand. 'I suppose Mrs Drage changed her mind and forgot she booked your car.'

'That's what happened. It stands to reason. I'm not saying she did it deliberate.'

Alice folded the cheque.

'You wouldn't think folks could be that forgetful, would you? Being as she booked the vehicle and when she saw me in the afternoon she reminded me about the next morning. The funny thing was she rang up again about five and said I wouldn't forget, would I? I was a bit narked, Mrs Fielding, I can tell you.'

'I expect you were,' said Alice faintly.

The incident of the car was a wholly unexpected development. Of course, it was possible that Nesta had forgotten. Her nervous depression had made her forgetful. But still Alice didn't like it. Perhaps she was growing forgetful too, for it was not until she was back in the High Street that she remembered her original purpose in calling on Mr Snow.

She paused under a shop awning and took her diary from her handbag. *August eighth, Saturday, Nesta leaving today. Raining hard.* Raining hard. She thought back to that summer morning, Friday, August the seventh, had been the last day of a long heatwave. She had got up quite early. The rain had awakened her and pulling back the curtains, she had said to Andrew over her shoulder, 'It's pouring with rain. The drive's almost flooded. It must have been coming down for hours.'

How could she be sure it was that Saturday morning? Because Andrew had answered, 'Nesta's furniture will get wet.'

If the drive was flooded at eight it must have been raining for hours. Helicon Lane was a long way from the station. Nesta wouldn't have walked. And yet she hadn't been there when Cox came at seven.

Alice began to walk slowly back along the High Street. She was building in her mind a picture and a timetable of Nesta's last evening. In the middle of the afternoon Mr Snow had taken the stuff, whatever it was, round to Feasts', and at five Nesta had telephoned him to remind him of the morning call. She must have used the afternoon for tidying the flat and preparing the furniture for Cox's. Then, soon after that telephone call she got out to make her round of farewell visits. Mr and Mrs Graham at The Boadicea, Harry probably—he had been her doctor—Hugo and Jackie, then Uncle Justin, last of all to Vair House where she had had supper.

Very weary she had seemed, more depressed than ever. It had been a warm evening and she had worn no coat over her thin dress of black pleated lawn. Her ankles, Alice remembered, had been swollen, bulging over the vamps of flimsy black patent shoes. She had gone up to say good-bye to Pernille and then she had come down and shared the flat cheese soufflé with them. It was soon after eight when Andrew had driven her back to The Bridal Wreath.

'Why not stay the night here?' Alice had said, for

Nesta, clasping her hand tightly, had looked so tired and there had been tears in her eyes.

'Too late to change my plans now. I've fixed up I'm stopping at the Feasts.'

That night they had begun shifting the graves. The very discretion with which it had been done must have heightened the atmosphere of ghostliness. From Nesta's bedroom window you would have been able to see the tarpaulin screens and hear the sound of earth being moved. That in itself would have been bad enough, but worse, far worse, the aftermath, when just before the first of the light, the coffins had been shrouded, abandoned, to await the coming of the vans. Of course she hadn't gone to Feasts'. Was it possible that she had forgotten that arrangement too? She had forgotten about the car, even though she must have gone to all the trouble of telephoning Mr Snow from a call box. Her own phone, Daphne said, had been disconnected.

'I'm stopping at the Feasts',' she had said, and her face close to Alice's smelt of a summer garden. Then she had meandered down the drive in front of Andrew, moving languidly in the hot dusty air.

Mr Feast was stacking cream cartons against a wall tiled like Covent Garden Tube station in khaki and white. He looked thinner than ever in his grocer's hat. She noticed for the first time a certain resemblance in that bulbous brow and hollow cheeks to Abraham Lincoln; the same crusading fire burnt in his eyes.

'I wonder if I might have a word with Daphne, Mr Feast?'

'If it's about the Freedom from Hunger, Mrs Fielding...' He glanced almost apologetically about his land of plenty.

'That's more my province, if you know what I mean.'

'No, it's something personal.'

'I hope the yoghurt's been to your taste. We've had to switch to a different brand, but it's very good.'

'Oh, yes, delicious.' It was strange that in the past few days sometimes the only food she could face had been the thin sourish whey in the green and white cartons. 'If I could just...'

'Through there, then.' He opened the door behind him and shouted, unnecessarily loudly, she thought: 'Daph! Mrs Fielding to see you. Go right up, Mrs Fielding. You'll make allowances, I know, for a certain amount of disarray.' She smiled, murmuring something. 'Did you want to take any yoghurt today? That's right. I'll pop it in a bag for you when you come down. Eat wisely and you'll live long, that's what I always say.' His voice, harsh and bird-like with a mechanical chattering note, pursued her up the staircase. 'The tragedy is that so many who would eat wisely if they only had the chance are deprived by man's inhumanity of the bare....'

Daphne came out on to the landing. 'You've got Pop started.'

'He makes me feel virtuous because I didn't go to the official luncheon.'

'Have a bit of something with me, will you?'

Alice shook her head. The half-eaten pork pie on

the tray without a cloth might be what Mr Feast called 'the bare' but the sight of it brought back a wriggle of nausea.

'You said you were keeping some things for Nesta. I wondered... Daphne, would you show them to me? Could I see them?'

'Them? It's not them, it's it. It's a sort of box. As a matter of fact Pop's got it in his room. He's using it as a bedside table.'

Mr Feast's bedroom was a long narrow cell that overlooked the High Street. Alice crossed to the window and looked down. The street was quiet, almost empty of traffic. Of course! The by-pass was in use, the plan was working.

'This is it,' said Daphne.

Alice turned. She could see only a single divan with beside it what appeared to be a table covered by a cloth and laden with magazines—*Peace News, China Today,* the journal of The United Nations Association—medicine bottles, an alarm clock, a green Anglepoise lamp.

She took a step towards it, then jumped violently. From somewhere behind her a bell began to ring, insistent, shrill, growing louder and clearer. Daphne glanced up and shrugged.

'It's only an ambulance. Some mad-brain's come a cropper on the new road.'

Only an ambulance... Why had the bell seemed like a warning. Go away, don't look? She watched the big white van turn out of the slip road, its blue light revolving. Her hands had gone up to cover her ears. She drew them down and gave herself a little shake, turning her attention once more to the table.

'But that' a trunk!' she exclaimed. 'A huge trunk.'

'I told you she left a lot of stuff.'

It was a wooden trunk, old-fashioned and long ago painted vandyke brown. Where a corner of the cloth hung was a hasp secured by a padlock.

'Is it locked?'

'I don't know.' Daphne wrenched at the padlock. 'Yep. I can't shift it.'

'I wonder whether we should. I can't make up my mind if we're justified. . . .' She hesitated and all the things that had alarmed her came back to her mind: letters which had never been received yet had been answered; the Endymion Hotel; the man who called himself Mr Drage; a car expressly, doubly ordered, that had called in vain.

'I reckon she can't want it all that much,' Daphne said eagerly. 'Otherwise she wouldn't have dumped it here.' Her eyes shone. 'Here. I wonder what's inside.' She pushed up the sleeves of her brown mohair sweater. It was less like a garment than an extension of her own shaggy hair. 'My God, it's heavy!' She had lifted the trunk by its leather handles and dropped it again, gasping. It made a dull thud on the square of matting by Mr Feast's bed.

'We could get a locksmith, I suppose, or perhaps your father.'

'Pop can't leave the shop unless I take over.' This Daphne was plainly unwilling to do. 'I don't mind having to go.'

'*You?*'

At Vair when they wanted anything done they sent for the gardener or Uncle Justin's chauffeur. If it was too big a job for amateurs a man with the appropriate skill was summoned from Salstead. Nobody, least of all a woman, would attempt anything as violent as breaking a lock.

'All you want,' said Daphne, 'is a screwdriver.'

Alice sat down on the bed and watched her dubiously as she came back with a toolbox. Daphne's eyes troubled her. They moved like a ferret's, darting between beaded lashes.

'What's happened to her, anyway?' The first of the three screws was coming unloose now. Alice shrugged. 'She's sort of disappeared, hasn't she?' The screwdriver twisted smoothly. 'Here...' Daphne stopped and glared. 'You don't think she's in here, do you? In bits, I mean. You know, like you read about in horror books.'

'Of course I don't,' Alice said sternly. 'Don't be silly.'

A wave of colic washed over her. The Feasts' flat smelt of sour milk.

'Here she goes,' said Daphne. The hasp had come away and hung against the brown wood. 'If it's anything nasty I warn you I shall be sick.' Her suet-coloured face showed two red spots on the low cheekbones. 'You look a bit queer yourself.'

Alice was breathing quickly now, clenching her cold hands. Why did Daphne have such horrible ideas? There couldn't be anything 'nasty' in the trunk. Nesta had been alive and well after it had been sent to Feasts'.

Daphne gave a snorting giggle and threw back the lid in a rush.

ꭍꭍꭍꭍꭍꭍꭍꭍꭍꭍꭍꭍꭍꭍꭍꭍꭍꭍꭍ **8** ꭍꭍꭍꭍꭍ

Aʟɪᴄᴇ sɪɢʜᴇᴅ ᴡɪᴛʜ ʀᴇʟɪᴇғ ᴀɴᴅ sʜᴜᴅᴅᴇʀᴇᴅ ᴀᴛ the foul taste in her mouth. She gave a quick depre-cating laugh. The trunk was full of clothes.

There was a black nightgown on top and under-neath it a layer of underclothes. Daphne pulled them out and threw an armful on the bed. Beneath were dresses, skirts, trews, a black and white check suit and four topcoats.

'All her clothes,' said Alice in wonder. 'Oh, but it can't be!'

Daphne was burrowing in the trunk. 'There are ever so many pairs of shoes under the coats.' She emerged, her arms full of shoes, packed heel to toe and wrapped in tissue. 'Look, Mrs Fielding, every pair of shoes she had. No, I tell a lie. She had some old black patent things. They aren't here.'

'She was wearing black patent that night she came

to us. I noticed them because the heels were so high and her ankles were swollen.'

Daphne dived again and came out clutching a flat case perhaps twelve inches by eight. It was covered in black leatherette and initialled N.D. Before Alice could stop her she had opened that lid as well and a sweet powdery scent tickled Alice's nostrils, dissipating for a moment the dairy smell. Together they looked at the array of bottles and jars, lotions, creams, green eye shadow and blue eye shadow, lacquer for the hair and lacquer for the nails, brushes for the lips and brushes for the lashes.

'It's what used to be called a vanity case,' said Alice.

'Fancy her leaving that! And all her best shoes and all her coats. Wouldn't you have thought she'd have gone away in her summer coat? Look, this white orlon thing.'

'Then which coat did she wear that Saturday morning?'

'She can't have worn a coat. She only had the four, Mrs Fielding. I know Nesta's wardrobe like I know my own. I'd been through it often enough. We used to swap clothes.'

'Then, what...Daphne, what did she take with her?'

'If you're asking me, I'd say nothing except what she stood up in. There' a black lawn dress missing. I reckon she was wearing that on the Friday night.' Alice nodded. 'What I don't understand is how she came to leave all her best things. She'd saved up for that check suit and it cost her twenty quid.'

'Why send them all here anyway? I can understand she might want a suit or a coat for the morning but she was only staying with you for one night.'

'That's easy. I told you we used to swap clothes. I reckon she meant us to have a good go through her things. You know how keen she was on black?'

'It was her mourning, Daphne.'

'Mourning my foot! She said she looked so smashing in the suit she had for her husband's funeral that she stuck to black ever after. If you don't mind me saying so, you are a bit naive, Mrs Fielding. Well, as I was saying, she meant us to go through her things. I've got a little black lurex number she'd had her eye on for ages, but when she didn't turn up I thought she'd changed her mind.'

'But what is she wearing now? She can't have lived for nearly three months in a cotton dress and a pair of court shoes.'

Lived? You needed clothes for living and if you were Nesta above all you needed the precious little case that smelt of musk and lilies and vanity itself. She closed the lid abruptly and as she did so the thought came back to her that for dying you needed only a shroud, a thin, black shroud.

'Unless,' said Daphne doubtfully, 'she got herself a rich boy friend who bought her a whole new wardrobe.'

In that case, Alice reflected wretchedly, she would surely have given the lot to Daphne. Certainly she wouldn't have tried to drive a hard bargain to get possession of the dress esoterically described as a 'lurex number.'

'Mucky lot of stuff she wore next to herself, didn't

she?' Daphne was shovelling through the underwear. Alice had already noticed how tattered it was, some of the garments hastily cobbled, most left in holes, shoulder straps coming away, elastic stretched and puckered. 'She was always one for top show was Nesta. I can't say I'm sorry I didn't get her for my step-mum, though it seemed a bit of a giggle at the time.'

'Your stepmother?' Alice was aghast. Mr Feast had seemed to belong to a different generation until she realised unpleasantly that he was perhaps no more than ten years older than herself. 'I had no idea...'

'Well, no. I reckon nobody had. We got to know Nesta at first at the Chamber of Commerce. Pop got into the way of seeing her home from the meetings. He was very keen on her but it sort of petered out. I don't know as I believe in marriages where there's a big age difference.'

Alice looked down, feeling the flimsy black stuff and hoping Daphne had not seen her blush.

'There were no hard feelings, you know. Not between me and Nesta, that is. If you ask me she'd got her sights set on someone a cut above Pop. Mind you, he felt it. Funny, you wouldn't think anybody'd be jealous at his age, would you? What d'you think I ought to do with the things, Mrs Fielding? There was a flicker of desire in her eyes as they lingered over the suit and the knitted coat.

'Hold on to them. What else can you do?'

Daphne must have misunderstood her. She pulled the coat round her and thrust her arms into the sleeves.

Horrified, Alice said, 'I didn't mean...' She broke

off and stood up suddenly. A lapful of brassiéres and petticoats fell on the floor.

Mr Feast was standing in the doorway looking at them, his face twisted with anger.

'**D**' YOU FANCY ME IN IT?' SAID DAPHNE. SHE PIRouetted clumsily and jumped when she saw her father.

'Where did you get all them things?' It must be a very strong emotion, Alice thought, to make him lapse into cockney. 'What are you doing with my bed table?'

'It's not your bed table, Pop. It belongs to Nesta Drage. We got it open and it's full of clothes.'

He fell on his knees among the piles of garments and began scooping them back into the trunk. 'Haven't you any respect for other people's property?' he shouted. 'That box was in our care. We're responsible for it. That's why the world's in the state it is, big people riding roughshod over the feelings of little people.' Stiff with horror, Alice backed away from him. 'Hitler and—and all that lot," he said wildly. His face had become a dark red, the blood pumping through raised veins. 'Swarming their dirty hands over the—the household goods of the people!'

With a little pettish gesture Daphne shrugged the coat from her shoulders. Her father grabbed it and clutched it against his hollow chest.

'Haven't you got no ethics? You're no better than a dirty little Fascist.' He crammed the clothes back, flung the cloth over the trunk and began replacing the copies of *Peace News*. 'Stealing her clothes, tarting yourself up... Now if you was in a Free People's Democracy—'

'Calm down, for God's sake,' said Daphne mildly. 'I'm sure I don't know what Mrs Fielding's going to think of you.'

'Mrs Fielding...' He seemed to see her for the first time.

'Come on. You're due at the Orphingham Branch at half-three.'

The name struck Alice like a burning point of fire in the midst of her swimming brain. Blindly she put out her hand, but it caught only at the empty air. She might have been standing on ice or in a quagmire for all the support the floor gave her. Her legs yielded at the knees and a great curtain of blackness, muffling and utterly silent, slid down over her eyes and her consciousness.

Daphne's voice, cheerful and excited, was the last thing she heard. 'Here, she's going to pass out!'

THE CHILDREN WERE SITTING IN THE CORNER OF the big untidy room helping themselves to Smarties out of a coloured canister. On the fireplace wall the huge green abstract painting seemed to be hanging crookedly. Perhaps it was only her eyes. The brightness of this familiar room hurt them, the red and citron chairs, the waxen snake-like house plants, the toys flung all over the carpet into which someone's heel had ground a strip of plasticene.

'Jackie...?'

'It's all right. Mr Feast phoned me and I brought you here because it was nearer.'

'Where's Andrew?'

'At work, of course. Where else? I phoned him, but you moaned something at me about not fetching him.'

'Yes, yes, I know. I remember now. I just thought he might...' Her voice trailed away. She tried to smile at Christopher and he stared back shyly. The crumpled dress felt hot and constricting. Suddenly she longed desperately for Andrew and the tears welled into her eyes. 'That awful man, Feast. He got into a rage, violent rage, Jackie, because we opened a trunk full of Nesta's clothes. I can't get his face out of my mind, those burning eyes and that lump in his neck.'

'It's only thyroid,' said Jackie placidly. Mark rattled the Smartie box listlessly. 'An over-active thyroid. That's why he's so thin and always brimming over with vim and vigour. I know I was only a nurse for about a year but that's one thing I do remember. Too much thyroid and you get like Mr Feast, too little — that's called myxoedema — and you get fat and sluggish.'

'He was going to Orphingham,' Alice said. 'Did you know they'd got a branch there? I didn't. That means he knows Orphingham well. Oh, Jackie...' She stopped, looking at the children.

'Go and get Aunt Alice a glass of water, will you?' said Jackie promptly to her elder son.

'Jackie, I think Nesta's dead. No, I don't *think* so. I know she is. I'm certain of it. A woman doesn't leave her home late in the evening or very early in the morning in a thin cotton dress without a coat. It was an old dress, Jackie, and Nesta was vain. No matter how miserable she felt she wouldn't go off to make a new start somewhere dressed like that when she'd got a new suit to wear. Besides, it was pouring with rain. I don't think she ever left The Bridal Wreath.'

'But the letters, Alice.'

'She didn't write those letters. For one thing they were typed. I never thought of it before but I don't think Nesta could type. All right, she signed them, but anyone could forge a five-letter name like that, particularly someone who'd had letters from her before.'

'But that means...' Jackie hesitated and forced a bright absurd smile as Mark came back slopping water from a nursery rhyme mug. 'Thank you, darling. Now you can go over to the playroom and—and *play*.' Alice felt too weak and preoccupied to laugh.

'Here.' She felt in her bag. The disgruntled faces brightened at the sight of sixpences. 'Go and buy something nice.'

'And for God's sake, mind the road!'

The two women looked at each other after they had gone, at each other and away again in the embarrassment that comes from an awful incredible realisation. It was impossible. Such things couldn't happen in a world that also contained nursery rhyme mugs and green abstract pictures and empty boxes of Smarties.

'Suicide?' said Jackie.

'They would have found her, Jackie. Cox's or Mr Snow would have found her in the morning. Besides, if she killed herself, why the letters?'

'You mean *someone* killed her?'

Alice drank some of the water and looked at the design of Jack and Jill on the side of the mug.

'Daphne said her father had been in love with Nesta. He was jealous of her. If he was jealous there must have been other men. I've got a feeling now that she liked to get a hold on them.' With a kind of outrage she shivered violently. 'It's loathsome, I know. I hate women like that, but that's what Nesta was. I've found out so many horrible things about her.'

'What sort of things?' Jackie said in a small voice. She kept glancing about the room, looking fearfully over her shoulder towards the door.

'She had all those clothes, but dreadful scruffy underwear. She had alopecia too, but I couldn't understand it when you remember her lovely hair. You used to nag me to do my hair like Nesta's.'

'You mean you don't know? The topknot thing of Nesta's hair wasn't her own. It was Nylon. Haven't you seen those switches hanging up in Boot's?'

Alice didn't answer her. She was wondering why she had always thought Nesta was beautiful. Beauty couldn't consist of false hair, plucked and painted eyebrows, skin that showed dry and mealy when the light fell on it. Was it perhaps only Nesta's own desperate seeking after beauty, her confidence in her own good looks—a confidence that sometimes seemed shaky, feverish—that made Alice believe in it too? Nesta had been taken at her own valuation.

'Alice...' Jackie found one of her coloured cigarettes among a mêlée of plastic soldiers and tea cards on the bookcase. 'What do you think has happened to her?'

Alice said slowly: 'She wouldn't tell anyone where she was going. It didn't seem so odd to me at the time, but it does now. It must have been because she was going away with a man. I can't help feeling she was killed by someone who was jealous.' Her eyes, roving across the room as she sought for words, fell on the framed photograph of Hugo on the sideboard. *She made a pass at me once.* Hugo had said that, but suppose it had been the other way around? Oh, absurd, stupid... Her own brother? People always tell lies about sex. She had read that somewhere and it had appalled her. Perhaps it had shocked because it was so true. 'Jackie,' she said firmly, 'tell me exactly what happened when she came here to say good-bye to you.'

'I don't remember all that well.' Jackie wrinkled her brows. 'You see, I was putting the brats to bed and she was in here most of the time with Hugo.' Alice sipped some water. Had they been planning to elope, those two? Hugo often seemed bored with his marriage, his children. From business associations he knew Orphingham well. She remembered how he had refused to go back to the post office. 'She was very upset when she said good-bye to me,' Jackie continued. 'She kissed me—funny, really, we didn't know each other all that well. Then she simply ran away.' Thin and boyish, her face white and intense, she presented, Alice thought, a complete contrast to Nesta. 'I can't think why she was so emotional about it all.'

'Perhaps because she thought we'd think ill of her when we found out what she'd done.'

Jackie shrugged. 'She went to Uncle Justin after she'd left us, then to you.'

'She was very quiet,' said Alice. 'While I was getting the dinner Andrew took her up to see Pernille. She came down ahead of him and I noticed she had to hang on to the banisters. I asked her if she was all right and she said she'd taken a couple of aspirins. I knew she'd been going to Harry about her depression but she'd told me he wouldn't give her anything for it. It was all in the mind or something. She slipped a little brown bottle into her handbag but I didn't take much notice—I thought it must be aspirins.'

'I wonder...' Jackie was suddenly thoughtful and excited, as if she was on the verge of a discovery. 'I wonder if it wasn't aspirin at all, but tranquillisers?'

'Harry had given her tranquillisers, or so she said, but they didn't do her any good and she wouldn't take them.'

'Someone else could have given them to her. People are such fools, Alice. I know that from my nursing days. They won't rely on their doctor but they'll take stuff that's been prescribed for other people. They think all sorts of drugs with awful side effects are all right for anyone to take. For instance, Mummy was taking some tablets when she was staying here in the summer—she's been feeling low since Daddy died—and she left the bottle behind when she went. Well, you'd hardly believe it, but Hugo wanted to take a couple just because some business thing had gone wrong. I soon put a stop to that. For one thing, they were the things you mustn't eat with cheese....'

'With *cheese*, Jackie? You don't mean it.'

'I know it sounds funny, but it's a fact. It's quite a fashionable drug, lots of people have it. I can't remember what it's called but it raises the blood pressure and the cheese raises it some more.'

'We had a cheese soufflé for supper that night,' Alice said. 'Nesta always had a good appetite but she didn't eat much of it. It didn't taste very nice and I felt awkward about it. After we'd finished she lay back in her chair and put her hand on her heart. She said her heart felt all fluttery as if it was beating too fast.'

'Tachycardia.'

'What?'

'Fluttery heart-beat. Go on.'

'Well, there isn't any more. I asked her again where she was going, but all she said was something about a holiday and then "fresh fields and pastures new". I remember that because afterwards Andrew said it ought to have been "fresh woods". Then he took her home. She was very unsteady going down the path.'

She hardly knew how to put it but she was too worried for tact. 'What happened to your mother's tablets, Jackie?'

'Don't know,' said Jackie carelessly. 'I expect they got thrown away. They aren't there now, anyway. Hugo probably slung them out. You know what a mania your family have for tidying up. Look, Alice, I'm not saying she actually took that particular drug —I *wish* I could remember what it's called—it was just a suggestion.'

Smoothing things over quickly, Alice said, 'I suppose practically anyone in Salstead could have had them prescribed. So many people have neuroses these days.' She paused, pondering. 'Mr Feast's terribly nervous and jittery, don't you think?' If only I dared ask Harry, she thought, recalling how sensitive he was about his professional honour. 'But, no. It won't do, Jackie. Nobody would know Nesta was going to eat cheese in my house.'

Jackie took another cigarette from the packet. The table lighter she picked up was fashioned ridiculously like a Queen Anne teapot. In the light from the flame her face looked wary and ill at ease. Wasn't she smoking rather more than usual, almost chain-smoking?

'Most people eat cheese after an evening's meal,' she said softly. 'You can more or less take it for granted. And, Alice—my God!—it was *Friday*. Nesta often went to the bread and cheese lunch. She told everyone she thought it would help her to lose weight. He might have given her the stuff in the morning, but she needn't have taken it until later.'

It was frighteningly true. And yet there was comfort in the thought that of all the three men Alice associated with Nesta only Mr Feast would have been likely to have encountered her that Friday morning. Mr Feast was jealous of Nesta—his own daughter had said so. He had a shop at Orphingham and would know the place as intimately as only a tradesman can. Besides, it was absurd to think of men as normal and matter-of-fact as Hugo and Uncle Justin stepping over the border of normalcy into homicide. But, if Jackie's hypothesis were true, Mr. Feast was already disturbed, his violent nature intensified by disease.

'Then Nesta was poisoned,' she said. Poisoned? The word had come out quite naturally and impulsively. What she had meant to say, of course, was 'drugged'. It was she, not Nesta, who felt this dreadful burning in the stomach, this movement of bile as if her whole being was constantly longing to reject something alien.

Presently the children came back with bags of potato crisps.

'Cheese and onion flavour,' said Mark happily, thrusting the packet under her nose. 'You can have one if you like.'

The smell of grease and, above all, the smell of cheese, was so nauseating that she quivered with revulsion. The child stared at her. Then, at a repressive glance from his mother, he put down the crisps and stood on one leg. Alice could see he sensed the tension between the two adults. The room was quite silent, yet with a kind of vibration in the air.

Mark was so like Hugo and like his great-uncle as well. It was as if Jackie had contributed nothing to his looks but just been the vehicle through which another Whittaker had been bred. Because she was suddenly ashamed of her suspicions, and because she felt that soon if nobody moved she would scream, aloud, she reached out and threw her arms around the child. It was a way of making amends, but Mark knew nothing of that. He struggled and pushed her away.

His rejection did more to hurt her and cow her than anything else. In it she sensed the scorn and dismissal of all her family.

'Why is Aunt Alice ill?' said Mark.

'I don't know,' said Jackie shortly. 'People do get ill sometimes. You know that.'

'Grandad got ill and he died.'

Alice wanted to cover Jackie's embarrassed giggle with reassuring, incredulous laughter. Her lips felt as rigid and as cold as pebbles.

'I'd better drive you home now,' said Jackie.

* * *

ANDREW DEPOSITED THE STACK OF NOVELS CAREfully on the bedside table.

'Are you sure you want to read all this stuff? You'll probably find it as dry as dust.'

'You don't.'

'No...' He smiled distantly. Couldn't he see that she was trying to create a new bond between them?

'Are all the Trollope politicals here, Andrew?'

'Not quite all. There are a couple I want for myself downstairs.'

Downstairs. That meant he wasn't going to sit with her any longer. Still, she must try not to feel even a shred of bitterness. A compulsive reader like Andrew had to read like others had to have drugs. Drugs... She shivered. It was unjust to admit the thought that he preferred reading a book he had read over and over again to sitting with his wife.

'Which ones are missing?' she asked brightly.

'Two volumes of *Phineas Finn*. It'll take you days before you get to them.'

'Days, Andrew? I won't be here for days. I'm going to get up tomorrow and go to the police. No, don't say anything. I've decided. I've got to do something about Nesta.'

Exasperation crossed his face and tightened his mouth.

'Oh, Bell! What are you going to tell them? Don't you understand you can't prove anything without the letters and you haven't kept the letters. Nesta simply tried to deceive you into thinking she was in Orphingham when she was really in London....' She shook her head violently and touched his arm, but he pushed her hand away gently. 'Of course she's in London. Try to be realistic. What you're feeling is hurt pride. At best your going to the police can only lead to your appearing in court as a witness when they find Nesta Drage and summons her for some paltry offense against the Post Office. And they can't even do that without the letters and without the re-direction notice.'

It was all true. What one logical reasonable man believed other men would believe. Only she and Jackie were convinced, largely by evidence that ap-pealed to the feminine instinct, that Nesta was dead.

Somewhere she was dead—and buried. The florist who had wound so many garlands had been buried without a wreath of her own. Where was she lying now? They had begun to move the graves that night and you could get into the old graveyard quite easily from the garden of The Bridal Wreath. The ancient coffins would contain nothing now but dust. Who of the midnight men moving silently among the yew clumps would notice that one was a little heavier?

If the coffins were too risky there were always the cavities left in the crumbly brown clay. A little could have been spaded away and later restored. A week afterwards tons of concrete had been poured over the rifled ground to make the slip road.

She hesitated fearfully, certain, but afraid to put her thoughts into words. Fancies such as these, spo-ken aloud in the still-warm room, would only serve to make her sound a neurotic. As she looked at him, straight and young with his smooth black hair, she was suddenly more than ever conscious of her age and that she was on the threshold of a woman's foolish years. She put her hand to her lips, then to the forehead that no longer had the satiny feel of youth.

He went coldly, slowly, without another word. She closed her eyes. When she opened them again Pernille was standing at the end of the bed with the yoghurt and some thin bread and butter on a tray.

'Mrs Fielding, I do not like to ask before because you are ill, but the stamps?'

She had forgotten all about them. A little half-hysterical laugh crept up and struggled in her throat. Stamps! Of all the trivial, prosaic things to have to remember when so many tumultuous things had happened!

'I forgot. I'm sorry. I'll get them as soon as I'm allowed out.'

'Kund will be so pleased. They are of more value when they are not postmarked, you see.'

Postmarks.... In the absence of the letters themselves, in the absence of the redirection notice, it might help if she could only say where those letters had come from and could show a sample of the typing.

'Pernille,' she said thoughtfully, 'd'you remember—Oh, way back in September—I had two letters from Mrs Drage?'

Pernille nodded, her clear dark skin growing increasingly pink. She stopped half-way to the door and looked back at Alice warily.

'You didn't happen to notice the postmarks, did

you? I thought you might have seen by accident
when you were taking the letters in.'

If she had been wearing an apron she would certainly have twisted it. Her face was a comical mask of
shame, guilt and self-justification.

'The second letter,' she said at last. 'I kept the envelope, Mrs Fielding. You had finished with it and
when I empty the wastepaper basket, there is the envelope with the beautiful new stamp. I look at the
date on the postmark and I know at once... Oh, I do
not know how to say it in English!'

Alice's mind went back thirty years to a rainy afternoon at Vair Place. She and Hugo had been sitting on
the attic floor and between them was Hugo's new
stamp album. Hugo had pulled her plaits and made
her cry because, anxious to take part in this mascu-
line pastime, she had wanted to soak a certain stamp
off a certain envelope.

'A first-day cover!' she cried. 'You kept it for your
brother because it was a first-day cover!'

Pernille nodded. 'It is the same in Danish,' she said
simply. 'You do not mind?'

'Of course I don't mind. I'm glad, very glad....' Her
face fell in sudden disappointment. 'But you've sent it
to Copenhagen?'

'No, I wait for Knud to come. Next week he comes
for his holidays and then I will give him all the
stamps I have saved. I long for him to come, Mrs
Fielding.' Not bothering to hide her emotion, she said
softly, 'I have been so—so homesad.'

'Homesick,' Alice corrected her gently. Suddenly
her heart went out to the girl. She had been too

happy with Andrew to notice this unhappiness on her own doorstep. Without hesitation she got out of bed and pulled on her dressing-gown.

'We'll go and find the envelope,' she said, 'and we'll have a look at your room. See if we can do something to cheer it up.'

Perhaps she hadn't devoted as much care as she should have done to furnishing it. It had a maid's room look about it, the floor uncovered but for the two stupidly bright goat-hair rugs. The curtains didn't match the bedspread and there were no ornaments, no books. Pernille's tiny transistor stood forlornly on the bedside table between a tiny brown glass bottle and a jar of hand cream. The envelope they had come for was retrieved pathetically from a writing case stowed under the Danish girl's pillow.

Alice took it eagerly and stared. It was clearly post-marked Orphingham.

But Nesta had never lived in Orphingham. Who-ever had posted it there had done so to sustain the deception. The three-penny stamp was one of the new issue of Forth Road Bridge commemoratives, vi-olet, blue and black. Its design of the great suspen-sion arcs beside the Queen's head was almost obliterated by the name Orphingham in the twin cir-cles of the postmark.

Tomorrow morning she would take it to the police. Surely they could deduce something from it, trace the typewriter, even find fingerprints? Delicately, as with tongs, she held the paper between her nail-tips. That greenish-pale assistant at Orphingham Post Office might even remember to whom he had sold stamps on that first day of issue.

'Pernille,' she said, 'I'm ashamed I let you sleep in this ghastly room.' Gratitude and hope were making her generous. 'I think we could run to a proper carpet, and would you like your own television?'

The pale blue kitten eyes met hers and looked away. Then Pernille smiled and nodded her thanks. Was it illness that made her see a kind of pity in those curling lips?

'You're eating properly, aren't you? Plenty of milk and meat and cheese?'

'I eat meat, yes,' Pernille justified herself. She shivered slightly, affecting disgust. 'But milk and that yoghurt you have—no, thank you.'

Smiling, Alice said a brisk 'Good night' and stepped out on to the landing. It was almost funny a Dane disliking the dairy foods that were so closely associated with her native land. She was concentrating so hard on keeping back the hysterical laugh that had risen to her lips that she failed to catch Pernille's last words. Something about cheese and lucky she didn't like it.

Alice went back to bed and ate some of the yoghurt. Everything tasted strange these days. Wearily she pushed it away and opened the first of the Victorian novels, seeing only a blur of print and line drawings.

The house had been perfectly silent but as she turned the pages she heard from beneath her a faint tapping, chattering sound. She listened. No, it wasn't coming directly beneath but somewhere from the other side of the house where the morning room and the dining-room were with the kitchen behind them. It is always difficult, she knew, precisely to locate the invisible source of sound. Then a door closed and quiet returned. The noise must have come from some of Pernille's kitchen equipment, for whatever it sounded like, there **was** certainly no typewriter in the house.

ʄʄʄʄʄʄʄʄʄʄʄʄʄʄʄʄʄʄ **9** ʄʄʄʄʄ

THE SUN WAS AS BRIGHT AS ON A SPRING DAY. THE
thick evergreen foliage on the bushes in the drive
gave a look of spring too, but along the edges of the
paths frost clung to the grass.

Alice turned away from the landing window and
began to go downstairs. The sun made bright flame-
coloured patches on the red turkey carpet in the hall.
As she reached the half-landing where the stairs
twisted before the final straight descent, she heard
voices from the kitchen. The door was slightly ajar.

'Of course she's years and years older than him.'
The voice was Mrs Johnson's, the subject of the conversation not difficult to guess at. Vexed, she bit her
lip and stood still.

'I do not know.' That was Pernille. Dear Pernille! 'I
do not think one would know that. She is so pretty, I
think, and she has a lovely body.'

'We don't say that over here, dear. A lovely figure,

or a nice bust if you want to go into details.' On the stairs Alice almost giggled. 'And she's got a beautiful head of hair, I grant you that. Always did have, even when she was a little tot.'

This was an instance of listeners hearing nothing but good of themselves. Alice took a step down, about to announce her presence with a cough when Mrs Johnson spoke again.

'Mind you I'm not saying anything against *him* . . .'

'Mr Fielding?'

'No names, dear, no pack drill. We know who we mean. Affection there may be, I don't doubt it. But as for taking him into the works that was a mistake. He's no more use to Mr Whittaker than the office boy.'

Alice froze again.

'Not that Mr Whittaker ever says anything, but you can tell from one or two things he's let slip. I'm a bit of a psychologist in my way, Miss Madsen, and I get to read between the lines. Every time there's anything in the paper about those schoolteachers wanting more money Mr Whittaker gets very hot under the collar. Scathing is the word. I said to Kathleen only yesterday, Blessed is he that sitteth not in the seat of the scornful.'

She could stand it no longer. Her grandmother would have burst in on them. Times had changed. Alice crept back to the landing and came down again, making an unnecessary amount of noise. Mrs Johnson's voice rang out loudly:

'I just popped over with an egg custard for Mrs Fielding, dear. Something light and sustaining. I'm not saying anything against continental cooking, but those made-up dishes are a bit highly seasoned when you've got gastric trouble.'

Alice opened the door. 'Good morning, Mrs Johnson.'

'Well, madam, this is a surprise.' Alice had known Mrs Johnson for thirty years. She had been a nanny to her, almost a mother. But when she came home from school at eighteen the Christian name had been replaced by 'miss' and from the moment she returned from St. Jude's after her wedding, Mrs. Johnson had begun to call her madam. 'We thought you were asleep and here you are dressed. Well, I always say it's better to keep going and not give way.'

'I feel much better this morning.'

'That's right, you keep going. When we had all that trouble over my cousin, I was that low, I can't tell you. Dr Blunden wanted to keep me under morphia day and night, but No, I said, I'll keep going with my usual....'

'I'm going out, Pernille,' said Alice.

Now she was on the point of going to the police, something held her back; reluctance to put her fears into words, perhaps, or shyness. The overheard conversation had been upsetting and she felt a sudden bitter resentment against her uncle. What right had he to talk about Andrew like that, as if Andrew were mercenary? Even in the wind her cheeks felt hot with anger. They seemed to be muffled in warm, suffocating cloth.

Postponing her visit, she went first to the post office and bought the stamps, then into the carpet shop and took away a pattern book. Harry came out of his surgery on the other side of the street, waved at her, smiled his sweet smile and got into his car. Outside Mr Cropper's shop the jeweller was standing in the sunshine, talking to Mr Feast.

'Good morning, Mrs Fielding.' He looked at her as if he wanted to say more, apologise perhaps, but she passed on quickly. The sight of him, cadaverous, intense, febrile, a jealous, violent man, was the one spur she needed. She went up the steps into the police station.

THE STATION WAS FAMILIAR BUT NOT THIS LITTLE room with C.I.D. on the door. The man on the opposite side of the table had a young handsome face creased with fatigue. She fancied strangely that so might Andrew have looked if his life had been different, without education and cloistered pedagogy. The face was like Andrew's and yet unlike. Fineness and grace were there but scarred, as it were, by the passing of a brutish hand in a rough glove. He had introduced himself and her heart sank a little when she heard he was only a detective constable.

She told him about the letters. His face was impassive. She told him about her illness and how it had inhibited her, preventing her from making all the enquiries she would have liked to make. Apparently listening, he asked her if she would smoke. Impatiently she shook her head.

'From what I've heard I think Mrs Drage may have been involved with several men. This is what I think happened: one of them wanted to kill her and he gave her some tablets he said were aspirins. But they weren't, you see. They were a drug that's potentiated by cheese. Everyone knew she went to the bread and cheese lunches because she wanted to slim. She didn't eat cheese that day until she came to my house.'

She stopped. Not until she was actually telling him had she realised that the meal which had contributed to Nesta's death had been eaten in her house, cooked by her. The realisation, appalling though it was, made her only the more anxious to find the truth.

His expression told her she had been talking in vain. Desperately she clenched her fists and brought them down hard on the desk. It was a mistake.

'So you've been unwell, Mrs Fielding?' he said.

'I'm not sick in my mind.'

'Nobody suggested such a thing. Don't you think being ill could have made you over-imaginative?'

'I haven't got a powerful imagination and I don't read sensational literature.' In her mind's eye she saw the Victorian novels she had left on her bedside table, but she couldn't smile.

'Well, if you could just show me the letters Mrs Drage sent you.'

'I've told you, I didn't keep them. I've shown you the envelope. The address is written down in my book. You see, it's like Sewerby and...'

'Yes,' he said. 'It's a very easy mistake to make. I know I've done it myself.'

'All right, suppose I made a mistake. Mrs Drage had never lived at Sewerby either. I spoke to the owner of the house and he'd never heard of her. Look, if you were to go—if you were to send someone to Dorcas Street, I'm sure that boy would tell you Mrs Drage hadn't collected the letters and the parcel.'

He corrected her gently, '*Some* letters and *a* parcel. Mrs Fielding, about the cheese and the drug. I'm interested in drugs and I keep a file. Would you like me to show you something?' It was a folder of newspaper cuttings. She glanced at them listlessly. 'The drug you're thinking of,' he said, placing his finger on the cutting he had been looking for, 'is a pep pill containing tranylcypormine.'

'Very possible, I...'

'It says here that if you take them with cheese they combine to produce a blood pressure rise which can be dangerous.'

She nodded eagerly. They were getting somewhere at last.

'Mrs Fielding, do you know how many deaths associated with this combination have been recorded in this country since 1960 out of an estimated million and a half patients?'

'Of course I don't.'

He closed the file. 'Fourteen,' he said.

'She could have been the fifteenth.'

He turned his graceful dark head from side to side in gentle incredulity. It might have been a younger, rougher Andrew sitting opposite her. He seemed to be growing more and more like Andrew every minute. There was the same black hair growing high on his forehead, the same narrow sceptical mouth. Suddenly she wondered if he thought she was mad. Mad women probably came in here and told him improbable stories. They would look like her with untidy hair and pale hectic faces.

'She wrote to me and told me her address.' No, that

was wrong. Someone else had written. 'I had a letter from Orphingham but the address was false.'

'If she wrote to you, Mrs Fielding, I don't understand why you think she's missing.'

'Won't you do anything?' she pleaded. 'If you could just talk to that man Feast, if you could get some expert to go over the envelope...'

He got up and stood by the window. She could see she had made some sort of an impression on him and she leant across the desk, striving to make a last appeal. His eyes flickered. Suddenly she realised that he was silent not from drawing conviction but out of pity and a certain awe of her clothes, her manner and her name. It would not do to cry in front of him. She bent her head and began pulling on her gloves.

'Mrs Fielding...'

'It doesn't matter. You'd better forget I came in.' She put the envelope into the pocket of her fur coat.

'We keep a list of missing persons. I don't feel justified in putting Mrs Drage's name on it at present, but we'll keep our eyes open. In case of any unidentified...'

Bodies, he had been going to say. In the face of such disbelief how could she tell him that they should exhume the graves in the new cemetery?

'I should go back home, Mrs Fielding, if I were you. I think we could find a car to take you if...' He saw the ignition key in her fingers and stopped. 'The chances are,' he said, hearty and relieved because she was going, 'the chances are that you'll have a letter from your friend in a day or two.'

His solicitude was unbearable. When a spinister, Alice had never seen herself as an object of pity. Now she was a married woman, but she felt that to this young man she was exhibiting all the traditionally sad signs of ageing spinsterhood, frustration, loneliness, a longing to draw attention to herself, a desire to make and keep friends.

When she had gone he would talk about her to the station sergeant. 'Bit of a nut-case, that one.' He might even tap his head. And the station sergeant, from a longer experience, would add: 'They go that way when they're getting on and they haven't any kids.'

Who else was there for her to turn to? Not Andrew. His reaction was like the young detective constable's, a mixture of pity and scorn. Uncle Justin and Hugo were at the works. Who but Harry? He would listen to her and believe. The police would believe him.

She must find him, go to the surgery now and go over the whole thing with him in detail. As she came down the steps St. Jude's clock struck one. Surely it wasn't as late as that? She looked up at the clock, half doubting, waiting for the other eleven strokes, and her gaze fell on the church hall, its doors wide open. Of course, it was Friday, the day of the weekly bread and cheese lunch. Harry would be there—Harry and Mr Feast. She must be brave and, if necessary confront him with something like bravado.

But it was the vicar who sat at the deal table just inside the entrance, taking the money.

'Good morning, Miss Whit—Mrs Fielding. Such a pleasure to have you with us again.'

She could think of absolutely nothing to say to him. Instead she felt in her bag and dropped a pound note in front of him. I pay grossly, disproportionately, for everything, she thought as she passed down the hall. I pay my way into everything and out of everything.

Daphne Feast was sitting next to the wife of the council chairman. Alice nodded to them, unable to smile. Father Mulligan was bearing down on her, slopping water from an over-full jug. She paused, giving him a pointless, supplicating glance. Didn't the Catholic catechism cite murder as one of the four sins that cried aloud to heaven for vengeance? He smiled back at her, a pale holy smile from a face like a rack-stretched saint's.

Harry was sitting alone among the posters at the end table. He tried to take her coat from her, but she drew it more closely around her, suddenly realising how bitterly cold she was.

'Harry,' she said, bursting into the middle of things, 'you must tell me, have you ever prescribed tranylcypromine for anyone in Salstead?'

'Have I what? Alice, what is this?'

'Have you? That's all I want to know.'

'Yes, I have as a matter of fact...' He stopped, holding a wedge of bread six inches from his mouth. 'Alice, dear, I can't possibly confide in you about things like that. You must understand that as a doctor...'

'Have you ever given it to Mr Feast?'

'Certainly not. That would be the last thing.... Please, Alice, will you tell me what you're getting at?'

'It's Nesta,' she said quietly. 'If you won't believe me I don't know what I shall do.'

He had seemed annoyed, prickly and pompous, because of the questions she had no right to ask.

While she had been the supplicant, a child with an empty bowl, he had been distant, unwilling to grant favours. Now she felt suddenly that they had changed places. Suddenly his face wore that look of hungry anxiety she had formerly felt on her own.

'Nesta?' he said, and then in a forced casual voice, 'What has she been telling you?'

'Telling me? Nothing. How could she tell me anything? Listen, Harry, nobody will believe me except Jackie. I've been nearly out of my mind with worry and Andrew won't listen to me. He won't talk about her.'

She was going to go on, pour out the details of her search, when he interrupted her with a remark so strange that for a moment she forgot all about drugs and letters and Mr Feast. His voice was practical and frighteningly kind.

'That's natural under the circumstances.'

At once she felt that she was on the threshold of a dreadful discovery, and at the same time that she was the last of all of them to make it. For a long time it had been there, a snake sleeping in a box, sometimes showing life but never venom. Now it was beginning to uncurl and to pulsate.

'What do you mean?'

'Alice, I can't discuss it with you. You must see that. When you married a man so much younger than yourself you surely realised there might be problems of this sort.'

The chatter in the hall rose and fell. A glass clinked. She pressed her hands together, suddenly very conscious of tiny sounds. By the vicar's table someone dropped a purseful of small change on to the floor. She heard the coins rolling and the scrabbling noise of someone groping for them. Her eyes compulsively fixed on pictured poverty, she said:

'I don't understand.'

'We'll come to Nesta in a minute,' he said, 'but, Alice, for you own sake you must stop connecting her with Andrew. It's essential for your own peace of mind.'

'Andrew with Nesta? I'm not, am I?' She could feel her voice becoming shrill, slipping out of control. 'I didn't know I was, Harry.'

His understanding and his pity was more than she could bear. She pushed back her chair and its legs grated on the rough surface of the floor.

'I'm sorry,' he said. 'If I hadn't thought you knew already I wouldn't have said as much as I have. You must forget it, treat it like a bad dream.' He put his hand out to touch her arm but the fingers caught only at her fur sleeve. 'Oh God, Alice,' he whispered, 'I'd give anything to take back what I said.'

Nor all thy piety and wit...nor all thy tears wash out a word of it! 'Let me go,' she said. 'I want to go home.' She pulled away from him and walked blindly down the hall.

ffffffffffffff **10** fffff

THE CAR ROARED ON TO THE VAIR GRAVEL. SHE was driving erratically, much too fast, and she saw that she had twice swerved on to the turf verges, breaking the edges and grinding down the grass. But she was home at last, home without giving way to the terrible temptation to burst in on him at the works, sobbing out violent reproaches.

'Are you all right, madam?' Mrs Johnson, aroused from silver cleaning by so much unaccustomed noise, reminiscent perhaps of rally driving and quite alien to the peace of Vair, was leaning out of a window. 'You're a bundle of nerves these days.'

'I'm just tired, And I'm cold.'

'You go straight in and get Miss Madsen to make you a nice cup of something hot. Nerves are very treacherous things, as I have cause to know.'

Alice leant against the bonnet of the car, almost

spent with misery and the need to make stupid conventional conversation.

A cloud of plate powder flew out of the window as Mrs Johnson flapped her duster.

'It's a pity you can't bring yourself to have a nice confidential chat with Doctor about it. I know he brought me untold comfort.' The unconscious irony brought a hysterical sob into Alice's throat. 'Now, if you'll just hang on a minute, madam, I can let you have just one thing....'

'No, no!' Alice cried wildly. If she looked any longer into that insensitive, nanny-ish face she felt she would scream. 'I'm going to lie down.' She fumbled with the lock, rushed upstairs and fell on to her bed.

Jealous. Whoever had killed Nesta had been jealous. A big man in Salstead, Daphne Feast had said. To someone with Nesta's background Andrew would have seemed like that with his academic past, his house, his Whittaker connections. But Andrew loved her, Alice. Of course he loved her.

Wretchedly she remembered the police station and the detective who, with his dark good looks and his patience that seemed occasionally to break into exasperation, had reminded her of her husband. He had shown her something she had refused to face before. Young men in their twenties *pitied* women like her, women who were approaching middle age and who had never been beautiful. If they were kind young men they pitied them, if they were not they laughed behind their hands. They didn't fall in love with them. Why had she never thought of it before?

But Andrew loves me, she thought fiercely, I know

he loves me. 'For your own sake,' Harry had said, 'you must stop connecting Nesta with Andrew.' All those evenings when Andrew had driven her home, all those weekends before they were married when he had been too busy to come to Vair.... He had already met Nesta then.

Why had he married her, given up the job that was his life, changed his whole existence, unless he had loved her? Because you are a rich woman, said a small cold voice, because Nesta lived in Salstead too.

When they had first gone out together he hadn't known she was rich and the signs of love had shown themselves at once. You fool, snarled the canker that was growing inside her. Everything about you proclaimed it—your clothes, your rings, the photographs you showed him of Vair Place. On the second occasion they met they had spoken to him of Whittaker-Hinton. She could remember it all so clearly and now she thought she could remember that then, at that very moment, he had lifted his eyes from the picture, smiled, touched her hand, begun to show her the marked attentions of a lover.

It was on his first visit to Vair that she had introduced him to Nesta. Beforehand she had arranged the theatre foursome, Andrew and herself, Nesta for Harry. But Andrew and not Harry had taken Nesta home. He had been away so long, while she and Harry talked desultorily about nothing, and he had come back talking lightly of flowers he had been shown and carrying a rose-pink cyclamen in a pot. That had been a present for her from Nesta, he said. A present—or a peace offering, a payment for services rendered?

She turned into the pillows with a dry sob that seemed to tear her throat.

H<small>E CAME HOME EARLIER THAN USUAL</small>, PALE, tired, his hair blown by the wind into Byronic disorder. She was lying flat on her back, staring at the ceiling.

'Why did it have to happen, Andrew?' she said stupidly. Her mind was so full of haunting pictures of him and Nesta, excluding everything else, that she thought he must know at once what she meant.

Apparently he didn't. If he felt any guilt, had any inkling of her meaning, concern for her drove it away. He came to the bed and bent over her. 'Why did what happen? What's wrong, Bell?'

'You and...' It gave her a physical pain in the mouth even to pronounce the name. 'You and—and Nesta!' She wetted her lips, shuddering. 'Harry told me.'

'Damn and blast him to everlasting hell!'

She had never heard him swear before. He had been pale when he came in but now he was white with rage.

'You were in love with her, weren't you?' she whispered.

He swung round, turning his back on her. He was a slight man, not broad or muscular, but now his shoulders seemed enormous, hostile, blocking out the light. She covered her eyes with her hand. With his soft careful tread he was walking away from her into the farthest corner of the room. She heard him close the door and a little metallic click, unnoticed a dozen times a day, was like a pistol shot. The mattress dipped as she felt him slump on to the other side of the bed with a heaviness that contained a world of despair.

'Andrew...' she moaned.

He would tell her now, confess, ask for her forgiveness, and at the same time admit what she could never forgive—a passion for the dead woman who had been her friend. Clasping her hands together tightly, she opened her eyes and waited.

'If I could only make you believe,' he said, 'how violently...' She let out her breath in a trembling sigh. 'How violently I loathed her! She was utterly repulsive to me. But you couldn't see it. I had to put up with that white slug of a woman with her false hair always around me because she was your friend. My God, Bell, I sometimes thought I'd strike her if I ever had to hear her call an anemone an *anenomee* again!' He shivered and she could see the tremor wasn't simulated. 'Those wrists of hers, so fat with a sort of dimple around them like a bracelet...!'

'Oh, my darling, why didn't you tell me? But, Andrew—there was something—something between you you wanted hidden wasn't there?'

'If there hadn't been,' he said dryly. 'I suppose I should hardly have felt the subsequent revulsion.'

'Tell me, then. You can tell *me*.'

'You remember that night we all went to see that play. *Rain*, it was. I remember afterwards thinking how apt of you it was to provide me with a Sadie Thompson.'

'But Nesta was invited for *Harry*.'

'You didn't make that clear, my love. You and Harry seemed to get on so well. I thought you were breaking it gently to me that here was the marriage of true minds. So, you see, when you asked me to take Nesta home I said I would. And when Nesta asked me in, all among the oxslips and the nodding violets, I went in. Oh, Bell dear, she made it very obvious she expected me to kiss her. I thought why not? That is why I was asked to this particular party.'

'And then?'

'Nothing. I swear to you, nothing. The next time I saw her I was engaged to you.'

All the time he had been speaking he had been waiting, she could see, for a sign from her. Now she gave it. First her hands went out to him, then the smile which had begun in her eyes spread until it irradiated her whole face. He got up swiftly, came to her and took her in his arms.

'Oh, Bell, I've been so afraid for us,' he said, holding her close. 'I wanted to forget it all—what little there was—but Nesta wouldn't let me. When we were alone together she used to speak to me as if we'd been lovers, as if we had some secret we had to keep from you. Then she'd say it might be better if you knew. I watched her disintegrate into the manic-depressive she'd become and I wondered when it would come out, the confidences, the lies, the excuses.'

She nodded and her cheek rubbed warmly against his.

'She was like that with Hugo,' she said. 'Andrew,

how many more were there? Why was she like that and how did Harry know?'

'I don't know,' he said thoughtfully. 'Overweening vanity, perhaps. As to how many more...Bell, I'll tell you something now. I felt I couldn't before.' He sat back, keeping his arm tightly around her shoulders. 'Back in the summer I was in your uncle's office at the works. You know how he always treats me rather like a minion?' She nodded, a tiny cloud passing across her new happiness. 'Well, that's fair enough— I'm not much good. He had to write a cheque for somebody. He just flung the cheque-book at me, asked me to see if there was one left in it, and went out of the room. As it happens there was just one left, Bell. I noticed some of the stubs—I couldn't help it. You know he uses a new cheque-book about once a fortnight, but just the same two stubs were filled in for payments for ten pounds a time to N.D.'

The initials on the vanity case.... 'That's horrible, Andrew!'

He said quietly. 'He may have been as innocent as I was.' Tilting her face up to his, he gave her a gentle passionless kiss. 'Don't worry about it,' he said. 'We'll never see her again.' He jumped up, springy and light, more carefree than she had ever seen him. "I'll get you some tea.'

We'll never see her again. For more than a week all her energies had been devoted to an attempt to see Nesta again, then to an effort to find who had killed her. Nothing had been allowed to stand in her way but her illness. Now she was almost glad of that illness. The last thing she wanted was to see or hear anything more that could evoke a plump tripping figure, eyes brimming with foolish tears, a black and white check suit seductively tight.

Andrew came back rather noisily and hastily for him.

'Oh, darling, it's a bore but your uncle's downstairs with Hugo. Apparently Mrs Johnson's spun them some tale that you're ill again.'

'I'm coming,' she said. She would have to begin putting suspicions out of her mind and now was as good a time as any.

The tea was already poured out when she entered the drawing-room. Justin Whittaker, his silver tie stiff as a sword pointing at and threatening to pierce his lifted chin, gave a pettish glance at her swollen eyes.

'What's all this I hear about nerves?'

Hugo handed her a cup of tea, slopping it slightly and cursing. 'I've just driven Uncle back from Orphingham,' he said. 'I was dropping him at the gates when Mrs Johnson came flying out in a tear saying you'd nearly driven the car through the garage doors.'

Because she could think of nothing to say, she sat down beside Andrew and sipped the lukewarm tea. Uncle Justin contemplated the ceiling.

'Ten thousand years of civilisation shed in an instant when you put a woman behind the wheel of a car.' He put down his cup as if he had seen it and realised he was holding it for the first time. 'What do I want with tea at this time of night?' he said to no one in particular, then to Alice, shaking his head, 'I don't know where you pick up these proletarian customs.'

She was about to make some angry rejoinder—

why were they here, what right had they to question her behavior?—when the thought came to her that her uncle's bluster covered concern.

'I was worried about something,' she said calmly, 'and I was tired. It doesn't matter, does it? I didn't hit the doors.'

'What you need is a tonic,' he said, 'something to knock all this nonsense about being tired out of you.' Reluctant to betray any emotion, he added brusquely: 'I may as well tell you, Alice, I'm worried about you. You've got something serious the matter with you and if Andrew here doesn't look to it he's going to find himself tied to an invalid—or worse.'

Appalled she jumped up and took a step towards him. Andrew was breathing steadily, evenly, not moving.

'Uncle Justin!' The burning pain which caught at her diaphragm was the worst she had ever experienced. It had come suddenly from nowhere and it diffused at once, pouring into her limbs and flecking brilliant, flower-like colours across her vision. Her legs had become numb and immovable and as she put out her hands into intangible voids, a spasm of sickness flooded her so that she could hear with her physical ears a roaring like the waves of the sea.

'What's the matter, Bell? What on earth's the matter?'

It was going to happen again, just as it had in the Feasts' flat. This time his arms were there to save her, but she fell so heavily that they both crashed against the loaded table. The last things she heard were Hugo's oaths, the shattering of china and the dripping of milk and tea on to the carpet.

* * *

SHE HAD BEEN CONSCIOUS FOR A LONG TIME, BUT there seemed to be no reason for opening her eyes. Blackness and withdrawal were all she wanted. She had been aware of comings and goings and now she realised that Harry only was in the room with her and Andrew. The two men were arguing in harassed angry whispers.

'I fully realise I'm not here because you want me,' Harry was saying, 'but since Mr Whittaker telephoned me, and Alice is my patient, the least you might let me do is try and make a diagnosis.'

'Considering you've seen my wife almost every day since this trouble started, and so far all you've managed to come up with is some mythical virus, I shoud think "try" is the operative word.'

'Listen to me, Fielding, a virus is the last thing I'm considering at this moment, but something very different. . . .'

'You make me tired!'

'Before I can be sure I shall have to make a very thorough examination and ask her some questions, so if you or Miss Madsen will help me get her upstairs . . .'

She felt his hand move under her arm. Then Andrew jerked it violently away. Still Harry didn't quite lose his temper.

'Come now, Alice won't mind talking to me. I think you forget she and I are old friends.'

'I've had about as much of this friend-patient stuff as I can stand. It's always been my impression that the less so-called friendship existing between a doctor and his woman patient the better.'

There was dead silence. When Harry spoke his voice was quiet that she had to strain to catch it.

'If anyone—*anyone*— but Alice's husband had said that I'd have had him for slander.' She heard him take a deep breath. 'For heaven's sake let's leave personalities out of this. It's essential that Alice should see a doctor. She ought to have tests made, a special diet.' He stepped back clumsily and she heard his heel grind into broken china. 'What on earth has she been eating? Did she have any lunch?' His voice rose and suddenly she knew what he was trying to say and why his voice had that chilled, appalled edge to it. 'Fielding, can't you guess what's the matter with her, or are you too much of an escapist to face up to it?'

'I happen to be a layman,' said Andrew, 'not a provincial, back-street physician. Now, will you please go?'

She opened her eyes then and gave a faint moan. Harry was standing, looking down at her.

'Alice,' he said, hardly moving his lips.

'I understand,' she said. 'I should have realised before. Don't worry, I'll be careful now.'

'I have to go,' Harry's face was miserable and anxious; his blue eyes stared down at her, wide with shock. 'Promise me you'll call someone else in, get a second opinion.'

'Of course I will.'

'Get out!' said Andrew.

He went without looking back and she saw that for once instead of stooping he walked erect. As the door closed she leaned back, the tears streaming down her face.

Now that the worst of his rage had passed he stood beside her almost humbly, abject, with eyes cast down. Evidently he expected her to reproach him, but she could think of nothing but the awful momentousness of Harry's words. *What on earth has she been eating? We must have tests made. Fielding, can't you guess what's the matter with her?* Harry was a doctor and Harry had seen, had divined from her symptoms, what was the matter with her.

It should have been a surprise and yet it wasn't. Subsconsciously she had suspected it all the time and that accounted for her fear, the dread which arose within her each time the nausea returned. Spasms of sickness had occurred at each fresh stage in her search for Nesta, or rather had occurred just before those stages were reached. Whoever had killed Nesta was frightened too, so frightened that he was prepared to make her ill, even to kill her, in his desperate effort to stop the truth coming out.

Harry would have helped her, but Harry had been sent away. Even if he had stayed there was nothing he could have done. Quite clearly there rose before her eyes a picture of them all as they had been before she had drunk that cup of tea, Hugo and her uncle watching her, waiting, talking to fill in time. The tea had been poured out before she had come into the room. One of them could have ... Oh, it was horrible! But how could she allow Harry to make tests, discover whatever it was—arsenic, strychnine?—and then incriminate her uncle or her brother? It couldn't be possible. Yet Andrew had said Justin Whittaker was paying sums of money out to Nesta. An allowance perhaps, or blackmail? Hugo had confessed to his own small adventure with Nesta. Maybe it had been not a small but a big adventure, an escapade that he would do anything to prevent Jackie discovering.

'Bell, we'll get you another doctor,' Andrew said at last, 'someone who really knows, a specialist.'

'I don't know. I'm so afraid, Andrew.'

It might not be either of them. Other men had been involved with Nesta. Hadn't there been something almost sinister in the way Mr Feast had pressed her to take the yoghurt? He had known that no one else in the house would eat it. She mustn't stop to think about consequences, about police in the house, endless questions, a trial at which she must give evidence, when her own life was in danger.

Perhaps it was too late. Perhaps the poison had already taken a grip on her from which there was no escaping except into death. As if providing an affirmative answer, pain suddenly gripped her chest, diffusing out in flowing branches of agony, and as she moaned and hugged her self with numb cold arms, she seemed to sense death's grinning presence.

'If I should die, Andrew...' She shook her head against his expostulations. 'No, darling, listen. If I die it's all for you, this house and, oh, ever so many shares in the works. And everything that's in the bank. I made a will when we were married and it's all for you.'

'*Die?*' he said. 'People don't die, my darling, because they have food poisoning. You're so tired and overwrought you don't know what you're saying.'

If only she could get up and call them all back, shout to them that they were wrong, abysmally wrong, if they thought she wanted to find Nesta now. All she wanted was peace, a return to the normalcy of last week, a body that no longer need wage a battle against something too strong for it.

'Don't leave me,' she said. 'Stay with me.'

'Of course I'll stay. Try and get some sleep.'

Then he did a curious thing. With the tips of his fingers he touched her eyelids lightly and obediently she closed her eyes. It was only afterwards, just as she was slipping into exhausted, stunning sleep, that her brain associated his gesture with the closing of the eyelids of the dead.

11

TOMORROW THE SPECIALIST WOULD COME. SHE had lain in bed for three days now and it seemed to her that hardly an hour had passed in which she had not rehearsed the coming interview, but still she hadn't made up her mind what she would say to him. Her association with crime, even though she was just a victim, seemed to have degraded her, smearing her with underworld dirt, and she pictured the distaste on the face of the great man as the truth began to become obvious to him.

The air in the bedroom was quite fresh—indeed she kept the windows open day and night in spite of the gale—but it seemed to her that the place was filled with a kind of miasma. Poison was in the air, in the mind of someone and in her own body. She had frightened Andrew by her refusal to eat anything that had not been prepared by himself or by Pernille, and frightened him more by her refusal to say why.

'I don't want to see them, I don't want them to bring me things,' was all she would say.

'But you could see Jackie, darling. She's made you a jelly and brought you some wonderful flowers.'

She reared up in the bed then and he flinched at her outburst of incoherent terror. And Jackie had gone away, hurt and indignant, leaving behind her a bunch of chrysanthemums with blossoms like curly golden wigs. Alice had always loved flowers and she had told Pernille to put these in a corner of the bedroom, out of scent but disturbingly within sight. They reminded her of the huge plumed flowers Nesta had woven into wreaths for winter funerals. Nesta had sat in her workroom with the chrysanthemums spread about her, her own golden head like an enlargement of one of the giant blooms.

Alice sat in bed, reading continuously, absorbing perhaps only one word in every ten, but turning the pages, keeping herself sane. Even so she couldn't keep her eyes from roving compulsively towards the vase in the corner. Then her body seemed to crystallise into a block of fear, a pillar of salt, while she stared rigid and terrified at twelve golden heads which the wind whipped and ruffled.

'When will he come?' she kept asking Andrew, for she longed for and feared the arrival of the specialist.

'Sir Omicron Pie?' Andrew always called him that, affecting to have forgotten his real name, and calling him instead after an eminent physician in one of his favourite novels. 'Tomorrow at three. You can't summon him at a moment's notice like some village quack.' And his mouth curled with a kind of scorn. 'How do you feel this morning?'

'I don't know,' she said. 'I wish I knew.'

The sickness which had been physical had undergone a subtle change. Now more than anything it resembled the dyspepsia that accompanies an anxiety neurosis. So many things could bring it on, the sound of her uncle's voice booming out enquiries in the hall below, the gleam of the golden flowers at twilight, her own thoughts that kept returning to the dead woman. But sometimes it came without provocation, mostly at evening or when she first awoke, and then it was so savage and unremitting that she knew no mental turmoil could have caused it.

'Pernille,' she said when the Danish girl came in with her lunch, 'would you take those flowers away?'

With only a hazy idea of what it had all been about, she closed the last page of the second volume in the series. Pernille rested the tray on her knees and she noticed the smart blue coat that was undoubtedly 'best', the white gloves, the black shiny pumps. For a moment the sight of those jetty pointed toes brought Nesta back to her so forcibly that she sank against the pillows, feeling a scented languid presence and hearing a voice whispering sad yet urgent words too far away to catch. Then, recovering, she said in a tone that sounded falsely bright:

'Are you going out?'

'It is my afternoon off, Mrs Fielding.' Pernille lifted the vase and held it in front of her.

'Are you going somewhere nice?' A pang of envy struck her. The girl looked so free, so happy, so radiant with animal good health.

'I think it is nice, yes. Today my brother comes for his holiday and I go to the airport to meet him.' Above the nodding blossoms her eyes sparkled. 'I am so excited to see him again.'

'Yes, you must be. Don't bother about getting back early.'

'Just think, I have not seen him during a whole year.' She hesitated and then burst out, 'Knud stays with a friend he has known at the university and...'

'Yes?'

'Mr Fielding said perhaps I need not come back till tomorrow, but you are ill so I...'

'Of course you mustn't come back!' A beautiful new idea was taking shape in her mind. 'Look, why don't you take two or three days off? Mr Fielding will look after me.'

'He will be home by five and all is ready for your tea and for your dinner.'

'You're an angel!' What could she do for this girl in gratitude for leaving her in solitude with Andrew? 'Pass me my bag, will you?' The notes snapped from their rubber band as flat and crisp as the pages of a book. Pernille's face flamed and her fingers crushed the green paper. She must be too overcome to thank me, Alice thought, watching her vanish in a flash of blue and gold.

It was ony when she had gone that Alice remembered what she had meant to ask her. 'Go downstairs and see if you can find a book of Mr Fielding's called *Phineas Finn*.' It couldn't be helped; she would have to go herself.

Pernille's bedroom door was wide open, tidy but for signs of last-minute packing. A crumpled scarf lay on the bedside table. Beside it she saw what she had seen before but which her brain had not recorded as significant: a small brown glass bottle. Nesta had been holding a bottle like that the night she died. It means nothing, nothing, she told herself, as the bottle seemed to grow to huge dimensions, filling the room until it glowed like a great amber coloured tower of glass. Pernille had been ill with homesickness. . . . Abruptly she turned her back on the room and closed the door.

Although it was still early afternoon the hall was already dark. The old sash windows rattled in their frames and the doors shook. Alice wasn't really cold but the sound of the wind, sighing and keening, made her shiver. The kitchen looked starkly clean and bare. Of course she had often been alone in it before, but seldom, she realised with a reassuring laugh, when there was no one else in the house. Her laughter echoed and she wondered why, all by herself as she was, she had made a noise at all.

Pernille had left the back door unlocked. Alice turned the key. She wanted to be alone, didn't she? The last thing she wanted was a visitor from the outside world, a malignant visitor bringing her some dainty prepared for an invalid.

Now to find the book. She walked softly into the drawing room and over to the shelves which lined the fireplace wall. Andrew had a complete set of Trollope and they were usually in the third shelf from the top. Yes, there were the clericals—from hearing him talk about them she knew their titles by heart—but where the politicals should have been was a long gap, just a stretch of blank polished wood with wallpaper behind it. Most of those volumes were in her bedroom—but where were the two parts of *Phineas Finn?*'

Andrew was fanatically tidy about the arrangement of his books. It was unlikely that he could have stuffed these two precious volumes among the modern fiction and the poetry on the other shelves. Just the same, she looked, whispering the titles to herself as her fingers skimmed their spines. But the two books were missing. All the time really she had known they would be. The milk chocolate and blue design on their covers was too distinctive to miss even with only a cursory glance.

He wouldn't want her to take the first editions. She crossed to the antique bookcase she had given him to house them. Dull green and gilt, attractive only to a bibliophile, they looked forbidding behind the glass doors. The key was in the lock but it had been turned. The books seemed to say, touch us not.

Perhaps the missing copies were in the dining-room or the little dark morning room they seldom used because it gave on to the shrubbery. Andrew sometimes sat in there by himself, reading, always reading. As she approached the door a sound behind her made her stop dead. It was a kind of whirring crepitation, dull but quite clear.

But she was alone in the house. *She must be*. Her nerves, already on edge by the discovery of the bottle, the unlocked door and the blank space where the books should have been, now seemed to prickle and jump as if long feelers had been put out to snag her skin.

The whirring went on, piercing her ears as violently as a scream. She kicked open the kitchen door, holding her breath. Then she let it out in a sigh and shook her head impatiently.

'You fool!' she said aloud, for it was only the refrigerator, its pump working noisily as it did perhaps once an hour, reducing temperature. That must have been the sound she had heard the other night, she thought, contemptuous of herself. How could she have mistaken something heard so often and so familiarly for the tapping of a typewriter?

The morning room was empty, cupboardless, with neither desk nor chest that might conceal a book. She came to the dining room. Bleak winter light flooded it from the french windows. She felt a sudden settling, a new ease. After all, it was just an ordinary November day, and here she was alone in her own house, naturally anxious and on edge as any woman would be under the circumstances.

The books were nowhere to be seen. The only explanation must be that, incomprehensible as it was, Andrew had taken them to the works with him. She pulled open the sideboard drawers, but saw only silver slotted into velvet-covered mouldings, tablecloths, their two napkin rings both initialled A. A magazine or a newspaper would have to do instead. There was a pile of these on a stool. Impatiently she began to shift the topmost copies and as she did so two heavy volumes slid out on to the floor and with them a fluttering spray of white quarto sheets and carbon paper.

Brown and blue covers, a little line drawing of bearded men sitting round a club table...*Phineas Finn*, Volumes One and Two. Why on earth had careful meticulous Andrew hidden them like this? But, of course, it was absurd to suppose that he had. He must have left them on the table, meaning to bring them up to her, but he had forgotten and Pernille, hurrying to get away, had bundled them up with the papers.

She tucked them under her arm and went to the window. Vair Place seemed to frown at her, a tough old man of a house, gaunt and impregnable among the beating branches. As she stared at the red brick-work, the white facings against which shrub fronds tore vainly, she wondered afresh if it was possible that her uncle could have done this dreadful thing to her. Her uncle or her brother? Tomorrow when the specialist came it would be too late to stop the whole machinery of police procedure. They would have to be questioned, any man who had known Nesta would be questioned. . . .

Any man? Suddenly she felt a renewal of unease that had nothing to do with Hugo or Justin Whittaker. Then, as if with a healing balm flowing into and blocking all the dark frightened corners of her mind, the idea which had come to her when she was talking to Pernille returned. Why shouldn't they go away, she and Andrew? There was nothing to keep them in Salstead, every reason why they should leave a place that had become hateful to both of them. . . .

She went upstairs dreamily, pulled back the covers and got into bed. It was ridiculous to spend all that time hunting for a book and then to be too tired to read it. She would sleep for a little while and wake up refreshed for Andrew.

* * *

'DO YOU TAKE MILK, MISS WHITTAKER?'

She laughed, carefree, ecstatically happy to be alone with him. Looking back, it seemed to her that the whole hateful business had begun at tea-time and now at tea-time she was going to end it.

'Andrew, shall we leave here and go away? Permanently, I mean. Would you like that? We could go tomorrow. I've thought it all out.'

'Sir Omicron Pie is coming tomorrow.'

'We could put him off, couldn't we? I know I'll be all right if I can only get away from here.'

'But Bell, what about Pernille?'

'I'll—Oh, I'll give her six months' money or something. She's longing to go home, anyway. She's terribly homesick. Darling, we could just pack up and go—go to an hotel somewhere. . . .'

He wasn't looking at her, but down at the silk bed-cover, the thick soft carpet, the shell-thin china on the tray. The expression in his eyes was so strange that for a moment she couldn't tell whether it was delight or dismay. His hands were clenched so tightly that great white patches showed on the skin where the pressure of his fingers had driven away the blood.

'Andrew. . .?'

'When we were engaged,' he said slowly, 'I came down here for the weekend.' Clearing his throat, he added carefully: 'My second weekend at Vair. I meant to tell you then that I'd have to take you away, Bell, that my work couldn't be here. But almost as soon as I arrived you brought me to this house. You showed it to me and said it was to be ours. Your face was like a little girl's, showing off a dolls' house, and I hadn't the heart then to say all the things I'd meant to say. We had lunch with your uncle. His face wasn't in the least like a little boy's. I know little boys, Bell, they were rather an important part of my life....' She started to speak, but he stopped her, shaking his head. 'He gave me a glass of sherry. God, it was as dry as a bone and I happen to like sweet sherry. But he couldn't know that since he hadn't bothered to ask. Then he said to me—barked is the better word—"We'll have to find a niche for you at the works, I suppose. I daresay you're not picking up more than twenty-five a week, are you, at Dotheboys Hall or whatever it calls itself?" The next thing I knew I was sitting at that enormous table with Kathleen spooning asparagus over my left shoulder.'

'Oh, Andrew, I never knew—I never guessed it was as bad as that!'

'I'd often wondered what it feels like to be a commoner married to a royal princess. Oh, it's very nice going on the Civil List, of course, but I confess I feel a certain blow to my manhood when the works foreman makes a slip of the tongue and calls me Mr Whittaker.'

'Why did you stand it? Why didn't you tell me?'

He took her hands and said almost harshly, 'Don't you know?'

She nodded, too ashamed to speak.

'Did you mean what you said just now, that we could go away and not come back?'

'Of course. It's what I want.'

Expecting him to kiss her, she waited, holding up her face. Instead he gave her hand an absent pat, and getting up, stood apart from her. He seemed dazed, like a man who, hearing the first tidings of unbelievable joy, cannot yet face or grasp them.

He would put the car away, he had said. Then he would see what Pernille had left them for dinner and bring something up to her on a tray. Or perhaps she felt well enough to come downstairs? He could put a match to the fire Pernille had laid.

After he had gone she remembered she hadn't touched the tea he had poured for her. It was almost cold and it had a stagnant look but she sipped it. She heard him lift the garage door and start the car. What was it Mrs Johnson used to say to her when she was a little girl? 'I always know I'm a bit off-colour, love, when the tea's got a funny taste.' She put the cup down and from the floor beside the bed where she had laid it, picked up the first volume of *Phineas Finn*.

All at once the house seemed very silent and stuffily still. A sound that had been part of her existence for a week now had ceased. Then she understood. While she had been asleep the wind had dropped.

For a moment or two, feeling a faint recurrence of malaise, she held the book unopened in her hands. The brown and blue cover was slightly torn. Andrew could bring her the Sellotape when he came up again and she would mend it for him.

If they were really to leave tomorrow she must make an effort, not just lie here listlessly. To see her reading would please him; he would understand that she was beginning to relax again, to take an interest in something apart from her own health.

Were Victorian women really attracted by husky men in Norfolk jackets, men with great bushy fair beards? She smiled at the delicate Huskinson drawings, lingering over them. Here was a winsome crinolined girl standing in front of a Gothic mansion and here a painfully real illustration of a hunting accident. The pictures were amusing but the text looked dreadfully political. How would she ever plough through all that stuff about the Ballot and the Irish Reform Bill? Besides the illustrations were few and the text vast, nearly three hundred and sixty pages in the first volume. She sighed. Like another Alice she wanted pictures and conversation.

Snuggled down in the warm bed, she turned back to the list of contents. The characters and the place names in the chapter headings were all new to her. 'Phineas Finn Takes His Seat,' she read abstractedly. 'Lord Brentford's Dinner', 'The New Government', Autumnal Prospects'. Her eyes were beginning to close... Then, with a little gasp, suddenly wide awake, she struggled up, first rubbing her eyes, then bringing the print close to them.

No, it couldn't be! It must be a hallucination, a delusion. She shut her eyes tightly and frightened by the darkness and the drumming in her head, opened them again to stare and stare. Every number, every line on that page swam together into a greyish blur except two words in italics: *Saulsby Wood.*

12

WITH THE DRUMMING IN HER EARS CAME A TERRIble swamping heat, a blaze comparable to that from an open furnace. Then the sweat broke from her rather as if an outer constricting skin was being shed.

Saulsby.

She looked at the page again and the print danced. There was no point in staring at it so compulsively. Did she think that by looking and willing she could work a miracle, change the name into something else?

Saulsby. She shut her eyes and slammed the pages together. Her body was wet, running with sweat, and her fingers left damp prints on the book jacket.

The names of the houses in the terrace in Chelmsford Road had been real places, but Saulsby wasn't a real place. An author had invented it for a country house. This wasn't a popular novel anyone might read; it was obscure, largely unknown. Only a connoisseur, an enthusiast would read it. She mustn't think along those lines, that way madness lay. . . . She pushed her fists into her eye sockets.

Others in Salstead could have read it besides—yes, she had to say it—besides Andrew. She began to feel dreadfully sick. Try to be detached, she urged herself, try to make a part of you stand aside and look at it as a stranger might. But who would know as well as he that she wanted to advertise for Nesta? He had known first, seen it all happen, because he was on the spot, here in the house.

You haven't any proof, she thought, this is your husband that you love. She had come up the path the first time she had been to Orphingham, and seen him sitting in the window reading this same book. Hadn't he shown her the cover then and told her it had been torn? It had all begun at tea-time and at tea-time it would end. . . . He had asked her the name of Nesta's house and she had told him.

'Saulsby. I've got it written down in my book. I'll get it.'

'Don't get up now. I know you don't make mistakes like that.'

Ten minutes before he had been reading it, per-haps reading the very name.

Bᴜᴛ ʜᴏᴡ ʜᴀᴅ ʜᴇ ᴅᴏɴᴇ ɪᴛ, ᴡʜᴀᴛ ʜᴀᴅ ʜᴇ ᴅᴏɴᴇ? In all her theories about Nesta's disappearance she had never yet been able to put a convincing face on the lover who called himself Mr Drage. It had been stupid to think of Uncle Justin or Hugo or Mr Feast. How could any of them have gone to London on all those weekends? Andrew could. Before they were married, separated as they had been by a hundred miles, whole weeks passed by when they saw nothing of each other. *Andrew.* Shock had delayed the action of pain. It struck her now as with a blow to the heart.

One part of her mind was wounded, agonised, the rest suddenly clear and analytical. It had been easy for him, a gift to an intelligent man. Pernille had been given tranquilisers—that was what the little brown bottle had contained. One white tablet looked very like another. When they had gone up to Pernille together, and Nesta had asked for aspirins, nothing could have been simpler than to have given her two tablets—or three?—from that bottle. And Andrew knew they were all going to eat cheese. Only fourteen deaths, the young detective had said, out of one and a half million people. But he had also said that this particular combination *raised* the blood pressure. Suppose Nesta's blood pressure had been high already? Oh, Andrew, Andrew...She stuffed the sheet into her mouth to stop herself crying aloud.

He had done it for her. To prevent her discovering his infidelity—had she threatened that very night to tell Alice everything as a parting shot?—he had killed Nesta. Could she live with him, knowing what he had done?

He must have loved her more than Nesta. What he had felt for Nesta wasn't love at all. Suppose it had been love but the lure of money and position was stronger? He had talked about being a consort, about going on the 'Civil List', but perhaps he had only married her to attain that. Rather than lose it he would do—had done—anything. If he loves me for

my money, she thought desperately, it's because I *am*
my money. I am what my money has made me, insep-
arable from it, part and parcel of it. A girl could love a
man because he was rich and authoritative and assured. Surely the principle remained if the roles were
reversed.

She would never let him know that she knew.
Everyday she would think of it, every hour. But not
for always. Time would take it away. After years had
passed she would probably be able to forget it for
whole days at a time. The great thing would be to
support herself now, tonight, just while he sat with
her and they ate their dinner.

Their dinner. . . . The words brought another rush
of heat and a fresh flow of sweat. The shudder which
took her jerked the bed and set the tea cup rattling.
He had brought her that tea and bent over her, smiling. A man may smile and murder while he smiles.
He had done it because he loved her. She tore the
sheets from her body and rushed trembling from the
bed. Why hadn't she seen the flaw in that argument?
Whoever had killed Nesta had tried to kill her. Nesta's
killer had tried to kill, or, at least, seriously to incapac-
itate the woman who sought him.

Chocolates, yoghurt, a jelly, an egg custard . . .
What a fool she had been! No one outside the house
would dare to poison food anyone inside it might eat.
But Andrew had brought her food and drink with his
own hands, knowing it would be touched by nobody
but herself.

She fell against the door, pressing it with cold
clammy hands. The foretaste of vomit was on her
tongue and bent double with an excruciating shaft of

pain, she remembered the foul taste of the tea. Suppose she died tonight? Harry had been sent away after an obviously staged quarrel. In her own innocence she had herself asked Andrew to cancel the specialist's visit.

Pernille was gone. Not she but Andrew had told her to stay away all night. Charitably he had sent her away so that he might be alone with his wife.

I must get away too, she said aloud. I must get out! With agonising slowness the sickness subsided. It seemed to draw away from her mouth and throat and travel into her limbs where it settled as a kind of paralysis. She stumbled to the window and wrenched back the curtains. Light from the drawing-room showed her the drive misted by a faint drizzle. The laurels and ilexes, still now after a week of turbulence, hung their immobile heads. Thank God Uncle Justin was next door!

She began to dress, clumsily and feebly because her hands were shaking. There was no time to plait her hair. She caught it up and twisted it into a coil on the back of her head, found the pins and stabbed them in haphazardly. A coat next. It would be cold out there tonight. She unhooked the fur from its hanger and seeking warmth, thrust her hands into the pockets. Something stiff and cool touched her right palm—Nesta's envelope, the first-day cover. The contact brought back humiliation. She had slipped that envelope into her pocket at the police station.

If he saw her on the stairs he would try to stop her. 'What are you doing, Bell?'

Nobody would ever call her that again. For ever

now she would associate the diminutive with sweet insincerity, a subtle, smiling poisoner. Clutching at her body, she let out a little cry of pain.

But it was useless to think of that now. For that she had all the rest of her life. Now she must get out. Cautiously she opened the door. The house was full of light. Down the stairs next as swiftly as her weak legs would take her. The front door, could she make the front door without his hearing her?

There was a light in the dining-room and she thought at once of the french windows which faced the side of Vair Place. From the kitchen came the very faint clink as of plates being moved. She went into the room and reached for the curtains to draw them away from the lock.

The room was different, changed since she had visited it that afternoon. Something, some unfamiliar arrangement of objects, unnoticed at first, but registering by their very oddity on her subconscious, made her turn towards the table. She started and froze. On the table was a typewriter.

A pad of perhaps half a dozen quarto sheets were in the roller. She moved towards the machine fearfully as if it were alive, able to transmit her actions to its owner by some method of supernatural photography. Her breath made the sheets flutter. Where had she seen that perfect, print-like type-face before? Methodically, as if she really were an expert sent by detectives to furnish evidence, she slid the envelope from her pocket.

The lettering, the spacing, the little serifs were precisely identical.

* * *

Like a second degree burn the shock it gave her was mild in comparison with the searing her mind had suffered from the sight of the words in the book. This merely confirmed what had been almost a certainty. Had he still hoped, still thought to quiet her by other means than poison? Had he been going to forge another letter? She stood swaying, not shuddering at all, but hollow and sick with horror.

Even when she heard his steps behind her she didn't jump.

'Bell, darling!'

'I wanted to come down,' she said, and every word was an effort. It was as if she was speaking an unfamiliar language. 'To surprise you.' But why was she suddenly laughing, a merry trilling laugh that bubbled out gaily? 'Yes. I wanted to surprise you, Andrew.'

It must have been the high strained note in her voice that made him stare at her like that. Or perhaps it was the fact that she had seen the typewriter. The movement he made to pull out the sheets of paper was swift and furtive.

Her foolish laughter went on unchecked. She couldn't stop it, though the feeling it stemmed from and it in its turn caused, was more like grief than happiness.

'Stop it, Bell,' he said sharply. 'Come and sit down.' She stiffened her body to prevent the recoil. Then she began to laugh again, but the spasmodic giggling died suddenly as his outstretched hands rested on her shoulders, terribly near her neck, pulling her towards the armchair. 'Let me help you down.'

Her will was too weak to hinder the great shudder. She shook and the coat slid from her back.

He stooped down and gathered it up in his arms. 'You won't want it in here.' Some of her fear, although wordless, had communicated itself to him. First she saw in his eyes apprehension, then he made a quick recovery. His tone was velvety. 'You surely weren't thinking of going tonight?'

'No. Oh, no, no, no. . . .'

When his hand—a dry, calm hand—touched her forehead and rested there she gritted her teeth and tensed all her muscles. Another moment and she would have screamed aloud.

'We'll have dinner in here,' he said, 'and then I'm not going to let you out of my sight.' Her teeth had begun to chatter. 'What's the matter with you?' Stern, unsmiling now, he had moved away from her, but his eyes never left her face.

'I'm so cold.'

He wouldn't give her the fur. It looked feral, alive, hanging over his arm, a prey in the hunter's hands. She identified herself with this old valued possession and she held her cold hands pressed against her cheeks as he went towards the door.

'I'll get a rug for your knees,' he said.

It was only a dozen yards to the cloaks cupboard. As soon as he was out of the room she staggered from the chair to the french windows and, her knuckles knocking against the glass, undid the bolts. In the obliquely slanted light from the table lamps his long shadow came in before him, heralding him. She sat upright and stiff in the armchair, clutching the arms. He spread the rug across her knees.

'You're to stay there,' he said, no longer gentle. 'You're not to move, d'you hear?' She nodded, terrified. Her head moved up and down, fast at first, then more and more slowly and automatically, like the head of a doll that has been wound up and is gradually running down. 'The sooner we get all this cleared up,' he said, 'the better.'

Only once before had she seen that hatred in his eyes, the day he had sent Harry away. Thoughtfully and deliberately he said, 'I'll light the fire.' He struck a match and the paper and logs caught at once.

Everything he did, she thought, shivering, he did well. The cold yellow blaze filled the corners of the room with flickering light.

'I may be a little while,' he said.

She heard him lift the telephone receiver in the hall and begin to dial. He pushed the door and it clicked closed but not before she had caught his first words. 'Is that Welbeck...?' He was phoning the specialist, telling him not to come.

It would be bitterly cold out there in the garden. She wrapped herself in the rug and edged towards the windows. The turning of the key in the lock made no sound. A dry sob rose in her throat but she was too frightened to cry. The door gave soundlessly and cold moist air seeped in to meet her.

13

THE EVERGREENS IN THE SHRUBBERY WERE WET
with black reptilian leaves. She pushed her way
through them, holding her hands in front of her face
to prevent it being cut by holly. As she passed the
greenhouse she saw in the blaze of light that
streamed from her own house, a pile of yellow lying
on the compost heap. It was Jackie's chrysanthemums. Pernille must have tipped them there before
she went out. Checked for a moment and breathless,
she stared at them briefly in fascinated horror. Each
with its golden curled head was evocative of Nesta,
dead, discarded, because its usefulness had ended
and it was in the way.

Only one light showed in the windows of Vair Place
and that was in the hall. She couldn't remember that
she had ever rung the bell before, always letting herself in at the back or by one of the casement doors.
Through the panes of glass she could see a glimmer

163

of red carpet, polished oak and pale porcelain. As she
waited the desire to giggle uncontrollably returned, to
giggle madly at colours and shapes and bushes that
poked spotted leaf-fingers into her face.

The door was opened by Mrs Johnson. Alice was
stunned now and she felt nothing, only that it was
funny and foolish of Mrs Johnson to be wearing her
winter coat and felt hat in the house.

'Where's my uncle?'

'Whatever's the matter, madam?'

It was surprisingly easy to smile, only difficult to
stop bursting into laughter right in Mrs Johnson's
face.

'Where's my uncle?'

'Mr Whittaker's dining with Mr and Mrs Hugo,
being as it's their wedding anniversary.' It was a sudden sharp shock, as salutary as the prescribed slap in
the face. Other people were doing things, things
apart from her; the world was going on. A wedding
anniversary—how funny, something she would never
have! But she clung to the newel post, not wanting to
laugh any more.

Mrs Johnson's eyes flickered over the plaid rug.

'Whatever possessed you to come out without a
coat, madam?'

'I'll just wait for my uncle. What time is it?'

'Just gone seven.' Grudgingly the door was opened
a little wider. 'As to waiting for him, madam, me and
Kathleen was just on our way to Pollington to see my
cousin Norman. But if you wanted to wait here we
could always cancel our arrangements. . . .'

The heavy feet in their thick suède-collared boots
edged back a few inches.

'No, no, not if you were going out to enjoy yourself....'

'It's not a matter of enjoyment, madam,' Mrs Johnson bridled. 'Only with Norman being laid up all these months, and Mr Whittaker being so good to him, I always feel it's the least I can do. Goodness knows, the Dawsons are an idle lot in all conscience and Norman not the least, but when it's a case of genuine illness...'

'It doesn't matter!' She stopped, putting the names together. N.D., Norman Dawson. Uncle Justin had been paying an allowance to his housekeeper's sick cousin. Another door was slammed, another question mark erased.

'Of course you must go. I can wait by myself.'

'There, and just this minute Kathleen's raked out the boiler all ready for the sweep in the morning. Half an hour and them pipes get as cold as charity.'

'It doesn't matter! It doesn't matter!' Alice cried. She could go to Hugo. It wasn't far, less than a quarter of a mile. She turned, shaking her head feebly, exhausted with the effort of talking. The door was held open just long enough to light her way down the path between laurels. She began to run along the street, stumbling and catching at the fences.

He would never dare to come after her. Or would he? If only her legs were less weak, the pavement dry instead of greasy with mud and water.

Your husband is trying to kill you. He had killed one woman and because you know too much about it, and because he wants your money, he is trying to kill you too. It was no good. They were just words, words that might have come back to her out of a book she had been reading. The facts were all there, clear in her head, but the magnitude of the horror provided an anesthetic that blanked out all emotion. Your husband is trying to kill you. Her mouth twisted into a silly smile.

Hugo's bungalow was the first of an estate of large modern houses built behind the elms in what had been a country lane. Lights glimmered behind a web of tangled black branches. She was going to spoil their celebration, burst in on a group of happy people just as they raised their glasses in the first toast. It couldn't be helped.

As she put her hand to the gate the lights of a car loomed out of the black hole between the arched boughs. It seemed to roar as it emerged like a train coming out of a tunnel and she flattened herself against the hedge, all the breath driven from her body. But it was only a shooting brake with a retriever gazing placidly from the rear window. Drizzle speckled on to her lifted face and a cascade of liquid mud splashed against her legs. This is how the hare must feel, she thought, afraid by instinct, but not knowing what it fears, running with hysterical leporine laughter.

The path to the bungalow was long, a causeway of crazy paving, slightly raised above wet grass. This was the last lap and it gave her a spurt of energy. She flung herself into the porch and hammered on the door.

Jackie was coming. Thank God Jackie would be the first to see her! With the sound of human movement, the certainty of immediate human contact, there returned in piercing violence the awfulness of reality. Andrew has killed Nesta, Andrew is trying to kill you... For a little while Jackie would hide her from the men, take her to her bedroom and warm her until the worst of the panic was gone. What would come after the panic she didn't dare to think.

The door was tugged open abruptly.

'Oh, Jackie, I thought I'd never...'

She gasped. There on the doorstep with Christopher in her arms stood Daphne Feast.

WEDDING ANNIVERSARY CARDS PROPPED ON VASES covered the mantelpiece. A big one with a slightly more pithy greeting than the others had been pinned to the frame of the lopsided green picture. A peasant, a displaced person with a blotchy white face under a cowl of tartan, looked back at Alice from the mirror. Christopher had begun to cry.

'They've gone to The Boadicea,' said Daphne. 'Didn't you know? It stands to reason she wouldn't want to mess about with cooking on her anniversary.'

The mirrored face mouthed out, 'What are you doing here?'

'Baby-sitting. And it's not funny round here. He's been yelling his perishing head off ever since they went.' She held the child out to Alice and stared at her. 'Here, you take him for a bit. If you're not in too much of a state, that is.'

It was as well the chair happened to be there. Alice fell into it without looking behind her. She clutched the child tightly, taking comfort from him. Diverted by a new face, he stopped crying. She pulled the comb from her hair and gave it to him. He fingered his own wet cheeks and then touched hers down which weary tears had begun to trickle, laughing as if he had made a happy discovery.

'Is there anything to drink?' Her voice sounded harsh, more like that of a hard-bitten woman propping up a bar than her own.

'I don't know. It's not my house.'

'There ought to be some brandy in the sideboard.'

Round-eyed. Daphne slid back the doors and handed the bottle and a glass to Alice. She dumped Christopher on the floor. He began combing the long mohair strands of the hearthrug. Alice poured some brandy and drank it. The comfort it brought and the new warmth staggered her.

'I reckon you ought to phone Mr Fielding and get him to come and fetch you.'

'I will,' Alice lied.

Fortunately the telephone was in the hall. She shut the door on Daphne. It was nearly a year since she had dialled this number, but she knew it by heart. Taking a deep breath, she waited for him to answer.

PERHAPS THERE HAD BEEN SOMETHING IN WHAT Jackie said. If she had done her hair like this years ago, taken trouble with her face, it might never have happened. Jackie's dressing-table afforded an array of things Alice had never thought of buying.

Busily she brushed her hair, but baulked at the thought of plaiting it. Instead she twisted it into a cone on the top of her head and with a strange excitement, stepped back to study the effect. She gasped, then in mimicry gave a tight little smile. So that was the explanation!

It was with a sense of indulging in a secret vice that she began to make up her face. The lips were a pale glossy pink now, the eyelids blue. As the final step in assuming another identity, she drew in dark arched brows over her own fair ones. The transformation was almost complete.

She couldn't go out into the road again draped in a travelling rug. Jackie's wardrobe was full of coats. Tiptoeing now, she slid one in black bouclé off a hanger and without looking back at the glass put it on.

The stage was set, the curtain about to go up. She opened her eyes and turned. Yes, it was just as she expected. Nesta Drage was walking forward to meet her.

She sat down heavily on the bed, euphoria displaced by shock. Had they all seen it, all of them but herself? Was that why Jackie had said, You ought to do your hair like Nesta's, because with a little juggling, a tiny change of make-up, she looked like Nesta? Her forehead was higher, her eyes larger than the florist's, but there was the same plumpness of figure, the same bud of a mouth. In spite of her illness, her face had filled out, heightening the resemblance.

Justin Whittaker had seen it. His affection for Nesta had been an uncle's, seeing in her the pretty womanly woman his own niece could never be. Andrew had seen it. He had married her because she reminded him of Nesta. Cold pain stabbed her and the face in the mirror responded with Nesta's look of melancholy.

Daphne's voice called her out of the nightmare.

'You all right, Mrs Fielding?'

She answered in a tone that was exclusively hers, cultivated and authoritative.

'I've borrowed one of Mrs Whittaker's coats. She won't mind.' Turning out the light, she stepped into the hall.

'Aren't you going to wait for Mr Fielding?'

'I expect I'll meet him on my way.'

'You do look nice. Quite with-it, if you know what I mean.' If Daphne had noticed the uncanny resemblance she said nothing about it. Her face was wistful, for whatever was going on she had played her small part in it and in a moment was to be excluded. 'Scared stiff you looked when you came in. Someone hanging about in the lane, was it? I thought to myself, She's seen some man and he's scared her. Was it a man, Mrs Fielding?'

'Yes, it was a man,' Alice said.

On the telephone to Harry she had explained nothing. It had seemed to her then under the pleasurably numbing influence of the brandy that once she was with him everything would ease and fall into place. He had always loved her and, seeing her husband with the eyes of an outsider, anticipating the inevitable, waited his own chance. He would take her away somewhere, somewhere, and one day, when it was all over...

She walked along Station Road, under the bridge, past the works, no longer afraid. In a moment his car would appear, swing in to the kerb beside her. 'If anything is troubling you—anything, Alice—you'll come to me, won't you?' But he was her doctor as well as her friend; she couldn't compromise him. For the time being all she could expect was a sympathetic listener, a friend when all other friends had failed.

Things seldom happen just as and just when you expect them to. But at the point when her thoughts said, Now he will come, the car twisted out from the High Street and swung alongside her. It was a little like falling in love for the first time the way her heart leapt. This perfect achievement of timing did more than anything to dispel her doubts. How had she ever thought him clumsy or gauche?

She was in the car beside him before she looked at his face. Then, as at last she looked up at him, his gaunt tiredness brought her a quick twinge of physical displeasure, and she thought visually of Andrew's beauty. Andrew.... Would she ever see him again? At some distant future time, sitting like this perhaps with Harry, she might catch sight of him far away, a stranger in a crowd.

'I'm glad you phoned me,' Harry said quietly, 'I thought you might. We began a conversation, didn't we, in the church hall? Perhaps we ought to finish it now.' He suddenly seemed to realise that it was night, that it had been raining and that she had walked. 'What's Andrew thinking of to let you...?'

'I've left him,' she said flatly.

She knew he wouldn't be surprised. From the first he had expected it. He turned the car into the High Street without speaking. The orange lights on the slip road and the by-pass lit up the sky with a dull glare. It was as if some horizon town was on fire.

'Harry, I can't talk about it now. I thought I could right up until I met you, but it's too near, too recent.

If you could just talk to me, be with me, till Hugo gets back... I don't want to be a nuisance, Harry. Perhaps it would be better if I went to an hotel. I just don't know any more.'

They passed The Boadicea. Hugo is in there, she thought. Hugo and my uncle. If she could not tell it to Harry, how could she ever tell it to them?

'I wish you could be with me.' Harry said under his breath. She began to cry. 'You'd feel better if you told me about it.' He gave her his arm and helped her out of the car across the pavement to the door with the brass plate beside it. In the waiting-room the chairs had been arranged against the wall and the magazines piled tidily. He didn't bother to switch on the light or lock the door behind him. 'You can lie down in here,' he said, 'and I'll give you something to calm you.'

Walking into the surgery in front of him, she saw her own reflection coming to meet her in the black rain-dashed window. At the sight of that gold and black blur she put her hand up to her eyes and sank into a chair. In silence he went to the medicine cupboard and handed her two tablets. The tumbler he gave her had about two inches of water in it. He had put on the light and the brightness hurt her eyes.

'Wouldn't you like to tell me about it now?' he asked gently.

She swallowed the tablets and took a deep breath. 'I wish I hadn't stopped you that day in the church hall,' she said. 'You were going to tell me, weren't you, Harry?' If only she had let him go on, not jumped up and run from him, she might have known it all before she had made those plans for herself and Andrew, plans that had been sweet and now seemed ludicrous. 'I could have borne it better, then.'

He was puzzled. 'I don't quite understand you, Alice.'

'Don't you remember? You said I mustn't connect Andrew with Nesta.'

'You haven't left him because of *that* ?' He gave a little dry laugh, Surprised, she looked up at him.

'That—and other things.'

He sat beside her and a tremor of alarm crossed his features. 'Alice, I don't know what the other things were—I'm not asking you—but I wasn't going to gossip to you about your husband.'

'What, then?'

Frowning, he said, 'I merely thought the time had come to tell you a few things about Nesta Drage. Oh God, I'd held out so long, but when you started to talk about her I—I braced myself for a confession, Alice.'

'Talk about her? Everybody knew I was nearly out of my mind with worry about her.'

There was no mistaking the shocked incredulity in his face. 'Why didn't you tell me?'

Like a jet of icy water the realisation hit her. He was right, she had never told him about it. Of all the people she might have consulted she had never consulted him, because she was afraid—with his swift warnings he had made her afraid—of discussing a patient with her doctor!

'But, Harry...' she stammered, 'Nesta hadn't been ill. Why should I ask you?'

Again the dry bitter laugh. 'Hadn't been ill! Did you think it was normal for a woman to get fat and lose her hair and be as depressed as she was?'

'No, but—Harry, I don't care about all that. I beg you to tell me where—where Andrew came into it all!'

She was calmer now. The tablets he had given her were taking quick effect. She bent toward him, gripping the table.

Suddenly he had the air of a man who, coming to the end of his world, may say anything, admit anything, because nothing matters any more. 'There were only two men in Nesta's life,' he said. 'Feast— and I don't think he was ever alone with her for more than five minutes at a time—and one other.'

'Andrew?' she whispered.

'Alice, I told you not to connect them. I meant it. Andrew, your uncle, they were just props for her ego. Believe me, you need props when you're a young pretty woman and suddenly, out of the blue, you get a loathsome disfiguring thing the matter with you. You need reassurance all the time—it's one of the signs. You want to be told all the time that you're still lovely and desirable.'

'What thing?' she cried. 'What thing? What was the matter with her?'

'You'll do anything to hide it,' he said slowly, 'but I think Feast sensed it. It might even explain the attraction, the drawing together of such physical opposites, one lacking what was such a burden to the other. I don't suppose you've ever heard the name. . . ."

A green picture, two children sent away out of earshot. . . . The difficult word Jackie had spoken came back to her and she faltered out the syllables.

'Myxoedema?'

'Clever of you.' He gave the ghost of a smile.

'But how do you know all this, about Feast, about Andrew and my uncle?'

'I made up my mind I'd tell you the lot once I'd started. You see, I was the other man.'

MECHANICALLY HER HAND HAD GONE TO THE telephone. She could only think, It's all right, I must phone Andrew. But he caught the fingers, stopping her. She was weak and his strength seemed suddenly great.

'Let me finish now. Don't desert me again, Alice. She reminded me a little of you, you see. There was an elusive something—like you in a distorting glass. I couldn't have you, but I had to live, didn't I?'

'I want Andrew, I must go to Andrew!'

Anger shook him. He grasped her wrists. 'Can't you forget him for a single moment? Don't you owe it to me to give me one last half-hour of your time?'

'All right, but...'

'We used to go to a place she knew—a sordid dump in Paddington. I think I'm shocking you, Alice.' She shook her head wearily. 'It had to be like that, secret, sordid underhand, because I was her doctor. Not very pretty, is it? Oh, I stopped needing her long ago, but she needed me. She used to say that if I left her she couldn't be responsible for what she might say. I knew she'd get myxoedema—how could I help knowing, a doctor and so—so close to her? I knew that if she wouldn't be treated for it eventually she'd become like an idiot, helpless, bloated, quite unable to look after herself. But she was so vain, and it didn't make any difference when I told her her vanity was just another symptom. She kept saying: "Leave me alone. I'll get all right in time. You're persecuting me because you want to get rid of me."'

To get rid of her. The words were like worms wriggling across Alice's brain. Suddenly she wanted to stop him, to get out into the clean cold air of the night outside.

'Please don't get up,' he said. She hated that near hysterical tone in his voice and beads of sweat broke on her upper lip. 'Let me tell you everything.' He paused and went on in a rush: 'She said she couldn't work any more. She couldn't stand the pace. With what she got for the shop she was going to stay at this place in Paddington for a bit and think things out. I could go and—see her there, she said. In a way it was a relief, but it was worse too. My God, I was frightened to death! Sooner or later, I knew, she'd have to get herself another doctor—she'd *have* to— and then, what would she tell him about me?'

'I don't want to hear! I don't want to know!'

'Sit down, Alice. Please!'

'I know what you're going to tell me, that you gave her a drug and she ate cheese and...'

'It wasn't like that,' he said in wonder. 'That wouldn't have harmed Nesta. It would only have raised her blood pressure and people with myxoedema have *low* blood pressure. Oh, Alice—poor Alice —is that what you've been thinking?'

'What was it, then?'

'I had a key to The Bridal Wreath,' he said. 'I was going to meet Nesta there the night before she went away. When she got back from saying good-bye to everyone I was going to make a final effort to get her to have treatment.' He hesitated. 'Look, Alice, I did try to get her to take thyroid. It's extract of thyroid, you know, that people like Nesta lack. I gave her tablets of thyroid and told her they were pep pills, but she wouldn't take them. By that time she wouldn't take anything I'd prescribed.'

The structure he was building up was growing to the proportions of a house in a nightmare, a house with many rooms through which you mounted until at last you came to the secret in the attic at the top. She wanted to get out of the house and run screaming down the stairs he was forcing her to climb.

'Harry, please...'

'I didn't get there till half past nine. I called to her but she didn't answer. Then I went upstairs and found her lying on the bed. All the bedding was packed and she was lying there on the bare mattress.' Again he paused as if afraid to go on. Alice made a little inarticulate sound. 'She was...she was unconscious. I didn't know what had happened, what she'd taken.... God, I wish I could make you understand what I felt at that moment. To be safe, to be free... One tiny push over the edge—not that even—just to do nothing and let her die. No one would ever know. Why let anyone see her, come to that? Acres of earth were all turned up outside. I looked at her lying there with that false hair coming adrift, and then I looked out of the window at a ready-made burial ground.'

A cry of sheer terror broke from her.

'What are you trying to tell me?' And her eye fell on the empty glass on the edge of his desk. 'No, no, Harry, no!'

She had come up all those stairs in the nightmare house with him behind her, prodding her on. The rooms had been laid open, one by one, and she had seen their contents, objects that grew uglier and more terrifying as each stage of the journey was passed. Now they had come to the summit of the top flight and there was just one door left.

Doors – the past weeks there had been doors everywhere, opening on hope, showing glimpses of black clothes and bright hair, and closing on despair. This was the last door and in a moment it would open too.

She backed away from him on the brink of a scream. He started towards her, murmuring something, very tall and bulky against the square window. Behind the door she could hear footsteps tapping, muffled at first, then coming nearer. It *mustn't* open. She had to get out, back to Andrew!

Was it the real door, or the one in her vision? There was a faint click as the latch began to move. It was an old door with a black finger-plate and a curly iron handle that crept slowly downwards like a snake, writhing and crawling across the wood.

Alice's stiff hands went up to cover her eyes. But they wouldn't close, instead growing wider, fixed and staring. The door opened an inch, stopped and moved again.

A little wind blew through the crack and with it came a cone of honey-coloured hair, a black pointed toe stepping over the threshold.

Her whole body had frozen into a taut knot of screwed-up muscles and nerves. Somewhere inside her was a scream that the back of her closed dry throat held imprisoned. Shock kept her fingers pressed against her forehead, but through them she could still see the bobbing blonde chignon and the black and white check suit. Between gloved fingers the initials on the vanity case gleamed out at her.

'Well, this is a surprise! Hallo, Alice. Long time no see.'

14

BENT DOUBLE IN THE CHAIR WITH HER HEAD
touching her knees, she knew that she had never
quite lost consciousness. The rim of the glass Harry
was holding to her lips chattered against her teeth
and water slopped down Jackie's coat.

There was a deep silence in the room. She was
aware of her own heart beating heavily. Then the silence was broken by the sound of Harry's lumbering
tread as he crossed to the sink, the gush of water as
he rinsed the glass, the nervous cough he gave.

The staring eyes were not Harry's. She lifted her
own and met them. A Jersey cow, a china doll, a
white slug of a woman—all those descriptions she
was now remembering, but none fitted the girl who
sat on the edge of the desk, looking back at her,
swinging long slim legs. Nesta was beautiful. Her
golden hair, framing her face in a cloud, blazed
against the old walls, the green baize. Surely her skin

had never had quite that translucency? She remembered it as strangely thick, always heavily *maquilée* Nesta was no longer fat, but slender. Instead of being like a second skin the check suit fitted as a suit should.

Speechlessly they gazed at each other. Nesta's silence, her lips parted as if she longed to speak but could not, only heightened the impression that this was just a vision. It was Harry who brought reality in to shatter the long dream. When he saw that Alice was recovering he went up to Nesta and said in a low angry whisper:

'It was inexcusable, creeping up on us like that. What are you doing, anyway? You're not due out till next week.'

Nesta blinked. Once she started to speak the words came tumbling out. 'I was as right as rain. They got fedup with me so they gave me the push. I thought it was the least I could do to come and see my devoted physician.' Alice could hardly believe it. This was Nesta; every word, every phrase, was hers. But this was Nesta as she had been when she had first come to Salstead. She heard her foolish giggle, watched the fingers in their long black gloves tap the desk. 'I popped into Feasts' first, though, and dolled myself up. I wasn't going to be seen a minute longer than poss. in that ghastly red mac you bought me, Harry.' Turning again to Alice, she smiled conspiratorially, all girls together, and added: 'Red, I ask you!'

Without knowing why, unless it was from relief or as a prelude to forgiveness, Alice put out her hand and found Nesta's. The little hand squeezed hers.

Nesta bent her head and sniffed the red rose in her buttonhole.

'I reckon I owe you an apology, Alice.' She looked so contrite that Alice shook her head vehemently. 'Oh, yes, I do. I've been awful to you and I've got a sort of feeling I've upset you a bit.'

'That,' said Harry, 'must be the understatement of the year.'

'But where have you been?' Alice found herself blushing. 'I thought you were dead,' she said.

'I very nearly was. Those last weeks in Salstead I was so ill I nearly went off my rocker.' She hesitated, then gave her hair a nervous pat. Glancing at Harry, she went on quickly: 'Something went wrong with . . . Oh, my metabolism or something. Nothing anyone could *see*. Mostly in the mind really.'

'Rubbish!' said Harry.

She gave him an indignant look. 'I was quite in a state that Friday.' The too bright smile made her thin-drawn eyebrows go up. 'It didn't make me feel any better, I can tell you, seeing the Grahams all jolly and bouncing at The Boadicea, and then Hugo and Jackie with their kids. By the time I'd got to your uncle's I was at a pretty low ebb. Well, I went into the kitchen to say good-bye to Mrs Johnson. . . .'

'And the silly old fool said she'd got just the thing for nerves and gave her a bottle with three Tofranil tablets in it,' Harry said. 'She *will* do it, hand out drugs I've prescribed for her to all and sundry.'

'She tried to give me some the other day,' said Alice, remembering.

'Nesta was a damned fool to take them.'

'When I'd been in to see Pernille,' said Nesta, 'I

went into your bathroom and swallowed the lot with some water out of your tooth-mug.'

'Tofranil lowers the blood pressure, the worst thing for someone with myxoedema.'

Nesta flinched at the word and Alice squeezed her hand.

'They have other side effects,' said Harry brutally, 'tremor, tachycardia, loss of appetite.'

'Well, I felt rotten when I got back and I thought I'd have a lay down. I must have passed out because I was nearly gone when Harry found me. I reckon I ought to be grateful to him and I am. They hadn't got a bed at Pollington so he whipped me off to a hospital in Orphingham.'

'*Orphingham*? You mean you were there all the time?' It was unbelievable, yet truer than any of her conjectures. While she had gone to the police, to the post office, while she had pursued one shadow at the florist's and another down the pavement, the real Nesta had been lying a hundred yards away at the cottage hospital.

'Harry came down to see me two or three times a week. He didn't want anyone in Salstead to know about me and I went along with him in that. Then he told me I'd have to drop you a line. You were going to advertise for me in the paper, he said, and I'd have to let you know where I was. The nurses might see the advert or one of the patients. Well, I said, of course I'd write but—I don't know, Alice—I was a bit unbalanced and I thought it might upset you to see me so under the weather. . . .'

'That's nonsense and you know it,' said Harry testily. 'She was terrified to let you see her, Alice. They'd taken away that hair thing she wears and they wouldn't let her use makeup. They couldn't have the symptoms masked, could they? She didn't want you or Andrew to see the bloated flabby wreck she'd become because of her own vanity.'

'Don't,' said Alice. She got up and put a protecting arm around Nesta, 'Don't be so cruel!'

'I got used to the nurses,' Nesta whispered, 'but it was bad enough having them poke and prod me. All except one. I used to have a bit of a giggle with her.' She sighed and lifted her head. 'She was a nice girl. Harry wasn't very sympathetic, nag, nag, nag all the time through visiting. As soon as I got a bit better he brought me a load of stodgy novels to read and he said I ought to do some therapy, learn a useful job for when I got out. My nurse used to buy me all the women's weeklies.'

'The upshot of all this, Alice,' said Harry impatiently, 'is that I simply lent her my typewriter.' Nesta gave him a resentful glance. 'Flower selling had been a dead loss, anyway.'

'I feel ever so ashamed, Alice. I don't know how to explain. You see, I didn't want you to worry about me, but at the same time I didn't want you to see me. Well, here goes. That nurse I told you about—Nurse Carrie—she said, wasn't it funny I didn't get any letters? Perhaps no one knew where I was. Why didn't I let her get me a redirection thing from the post office and have my stuff sent on to the hospital from Salstead? She said she didn't like to think of anyone not getting any letters. It reminded her of an old man who lived at a house called Sewerby in Chelmsford Road next door but one to her mum. He never got any letters, she said, and when he went into the post office for his pension he'd seen a notice that said *Someone, somewhere, wants a letter from you* and it had cut him to the heart. She laughed then and said it was a chance anyhow whether anyone in Chelmsford Road got their letters or not on account of the new postman being more or less half-witted.'

'Oh, Nesta!' Alice cried and she began to laugh weakly.

'You know me, Alice. I always was one for puzzles, crosswords, quizzes, something to occupy the mind.'

'Go on,' said Harry.

'*All right.* Only I want to tell it my way, d'you mind? I filled up the form, Alice, and put Sewerby as my last address.' Alice looked at her, but didn't interrupt. 'I thought I'd have the stuff sent on to the hospital—I did mean to, I swear I did—but then I thought, my God, Nurse Currie'll bring in my post and she'll see the Sewerby address, next door but one to her own mother, Alice, and then where'll I be? So I fixed on the Endymion. You see I knew they'd be safe there and I could pop up and fetch them when I got out. They were always saying, you'll be out in a week or two, Mrs Drage. How was I to know you'd keep writing and get all steamed up?'

'You did your best to stop me,' Alice said. 'Your letters weren't very encouraging.'

'That wasn't intentional, duckie. I never could get the hang of that machine. Just a few lines and that was about my limit. But, look, Alice, you're not to blame Harry. I never told him a thing.'

'I don't understand how you knew your plan was

working. Nesta. I mean, the postman might have seen through it. I mightn't have sent off the ring...'

'That was where Harry came in. He hadn't seen you but he'd got wind of it by the old grapevine.'

Harry interrupted savagely, 'Let me tell her, will you? I met your sister-in-law, Alice. She said you'd been writing to Nesta. I didn't know the details and I didn't want to. I left it at that. You do see, don't you?'

Alice saw. He would have been too frightened, too apprehensive of the outcome to ask any questions.

'Nesta said she couldn't get on with the typing,' he went on, 'so I fetched the machine away. Andrew had told me he needed one and I took it in to him that day you came down to Orphingham. God knows I can't stand him—what's the use pretending?—but I couldn't bear to think of him spending any more of your money. That car, that watch you gave him—I wasn't going to sit by and see him squander a hundred pounds on another expensive toy!'

She felt herself grow white with anger, but she set her teeth. When she spoke the rage vibrated through the mild words. 'You don't understand, Harry, you don't begin to understand...'

'I'm sorry. I shouldn't have said that. Never mind, skip it, forget it. Andrew told me you'd gone to Orphingham to look for Nesta. He said she was living here—living in a private house, I mean. God, I didn't know what was going on. I'd brought him back a book I'd borrowed—Nesta had been reading it—and I just dropped it on the table, muttered something about having to get down to the surgery and got out. Then, the next day I saw you at the bread and cheese lunch. You said you'd been looking for Nesta and you started asking Daphne Feast. I was going to tell you where Nesta was then, Alice, but there were all those people there—that damned woman wanted to talk to me about her diet... I said you were to come to me if anything was troubling you. It was a hint to come and see me by yourself, but you didn't come and...'

'And then I told him,' said Nesta, 'made a clean breast of the whole thing.' She giggled. 'They say open confession is good for the soul. My God, I thought he'd do me an injury, he was so mad. When I said all the stuff was going to the Endrymion he nearly had a fit.'

'I went up and got the letters,' Harry muttered. 'I couldn't tell you about it after that, Alice. You'd have told Andrew and he'd have had me up before the Medical Council. I could just see it. Mr Drage, otherwise Dr Blunden, spending weekends with a patient in an hotel, and what an hotel!'

Nesta looked demurely down at her black gloves. 'Poor Harry would have been struck off,' she said. 'Can you picture him, Alice, all down at heel, peddling patent medicines from door to door? That's what happens to doctors who go off the rails. I've seen it on TV.'

'Oh, shut up!' said Hary. He turned to Alice. 'Once I'd got the letters, Alice, I thought it would all blow over. But when you started connecting Andrew with Nesta I knew I'd have to set things straight.'

'You don't have to go on,' said Alice. 'I can see it all, but for one thing. If you meant to give your address as Sewerby, Nesta, why didn't you?'

'I did. Of course I did.'

Her bewilderment was momentary. 'Did you enjoy *Phineas Finn*, Nesta?' she asked dryly.

'Did I what?'

'A Victorian novel with a blue and brown cover.'

'You mean Andrew's book? There are limits, Alice. I reckon Harry must have thought he was improving my mind. I flipped through it and had a look at the pictures and, believe me, that was enough.'

'Enough to make you have a mental aberration and write Saulsby when you meant Sewerby,' Recalling the young detective's words, she said softly, 'It's an easy mistake to make.'

Nesta put her hand up to her mouth. At last she said, 'No wonder I couldn't ever get those crosswords to come out.'

'I'll take you home, Alice,' said Harry wearily. He felt in his pocket and held out his hand to Nesta. Something in his palm winked and glittered as diamond chips caught the light. 'By the way, I've had this for a week. I forgot to give it to you.'

Slowly Nesta drew the black glove off her left hand. Then she waved her third finger slowly.

'Somehow I don't think I'm going to need it.' The black diamond was large, square-cut and expensive-looking. 'My fiancé—oh, you don't know, do you?— he's quite a big man in his way. He broke his leg when his Jag ran into a lorry the first day the by-pass opened.' She laughed as they stared at her. Alice was remembering the ambulance she had heard that day at Feasts', and wondered strangely in the midst of the other greater wonder. That was the day she had first believed Nesta dead. Had the ambulance in fact been bringing her a new life? 'Of course he had a private room at Orphingham,' Nesta went on, 'but they've got a lovely lounge there—for the first—and second-class passengers.' She giggled at her own joke. 'I've only known him a week. It's what they call a whirl-wind romance. Don't look like that, Harry. I shan't tell him about you.' She drew on her glove and in a queer little gesture of hope, pressed both index fingers along the painted hairless lines of her brows. 'I've got something to lose now, too,' she said.

'I CAN'T UNDERSTAND WHY I WAS SO SURE SHE WAS dead.'

'Perhaps you wished she was,' Harry said quietly.

'I wished Nesta was dead? But that's nonsense, that's horrible! I spent days and weeks looking for her. I was nearly out of my mind with worry. I spent pounds and pounds trying to find her.'

'Why did you try to make yourself look like her tonight?'

'I . . .' Why had she? She put her handkerchief up to her eyes and scrubbed at the blue on the lids.

He said impatiently: 'You're not really alike, you know. What you see in the mirror isn't the true image. It's lateral inversion. It's not what other people see, Alice. I believe you looked in the mirror and sometimes you saw her as if she were the other side of yourself.' She stared at him as he turned into Station Road and stopped the car. Then he turned to face her. 'You see, Nesta had succeeded where you had failed, Alice. You were a spinster at thirty-seven, rich but without a career. Nesta had married young, earned her own living, made herself attractive to men. It was only when she started to get ill that you really took her up.'

'I was *sorry* for her.'

'Perhaps you were. You weren't sorry for yourself any more because you were going to be married. Then Nesta moved away and disappeared. By then you'd changed places, but you didn't quite want to lose the other self that was lonely, just as you had been. Money would get her back just as money had got you everything.'

'No!' she cried. 'No, Harry, it isn't true.'

'Why not be detached about it? We all act this way. You began to find things out about her, the way she had attracted Andrew. Perhaps she'd been attractive to other people as well.' Alice put her hands up to her face. 'You were going to kill that other image with all the things it implied, particularly Andrew's infidelity.' With swift intuition, he added: 'Bury it deep in the coffins and make way for a new road. Maybe you had killed her. Where else did you get that mad idea about the cheese? Or if you hadn't Andrew had. Andrew had killed the young, the pretty, the desirable.'

'How you must hate me, Harry,' she said.

'Hatred, as Nesta might say, is akin to love.'

'Not your kind of hatred. Whatever Nesta was going to tell me about it was enough to make you go to any lengths.' She sobbed and wrenched at the car door. 'Look, I can forgive you if you were only trying to make me ill, but . . . Why did you poison me? Why?'

She was breathing deeply, sobbing as she caught each breath. What he would do she hardly knew, but the orgy of fear she had experienced at Vair and afterwards at the surgery—a fear that had been none the less real because she now knew it was unnecessary —had left her indifferent to further terror.

As she was about to step out, he touched her arm. The question he asked her was totally unexpected, inconsequential, under the circumstances an insult.

'What d'you think? You talk to me about worry. How do you think it's been for me, ill, terrified to eat, suspecting everyone I loved of trying to kill me?'

'You aren't ill,' he said, 'and nobody's been trying to poison you. You're going to have a child.'

She SAID NOTHING. BUT SHE GOT OUT OF THE CAR. The air was cold and fresh. She leant against one of the wings and began to cry.

Presently he came out and stood beside her.

'I didn't know at first,' he said, 'but I guessed that day at the lunch when you got into such a state. When you fainted and I came up to Vair I wanted to examine you and make sure, but Andrew wouldn't let me.' He sighed heavily. 'I was glad in a way. You see, when you're in love with someone and she marries someone else the only way you can stop yourself going off your head is by self-deception. You can't face up to the facts and you tell yourself it's for companionship—what does the prayer book say?—the mutual society the one ought to have of the other. In your heart you know it isn't, it's a true marriage in every sense of the word, but you fool yourself, you get used to it and you achieve a kind of acquiescence.'

He looked at her as if he would have liked to take her hand. But she stood stunned, swaying a little, letting the wind play on her face.

'Then something else happens, what's happened to you. I couldn't fool myself any longer. I felt ten times worse than I did the day you told me you were engaged to him. It was as if the fact of the marriage had really been brought home to me at last. But I didn't want to have to tell you. The specialist could do that.' He gave a dry laugh. 'As if it needed a specialist! Any half-baked midwife could have seen it—the way you walked, the way your face had filled out and made you look ten years younger, that sickness. Why do you think you had all those fantastic ideas about Nesta? Didn't it ever occur to you—doesn't it now— that they were just the fancies of an imagination heightened by pregnancy?'

Still she was speechless. A thin rain had begun to fall, little more than a heavy mist. The cloying air was almost unbreathable. It dewed her face.

'Let someone else tell them, I thought. I knew I couldn't bear to see your happiness and his.' His voice broke and he cleared his throat. 'To see it,' he said, 'and to know it had nothing whatsoever to do with me.'

'I am happy,' she said.

She drew the black coat around her and pressed her hands to her waist. Happiness spiralled through her and seemed to burst into flower.

'Let's go,' he said.

'No.'

His eyelids fell and she looked into a face that was blank and blind.

'I'm going to telephone Andrew and get him to fetch me.'

'Andrew!' he said bitterly. 'Always Andrew. Funny, I

always hoped, Alice. I thought it would only be a matter of time. He'd leave you and then—then you'd come to me.'

'Andrew will never leave me,' she said sternly.

She walked away from him quite fast, not looking back at all. The telephone box on the corner of High Street and the slip road was empty. A gang of youths loitered outside The Boadicea and although her hair was coming down and she had bitten most of Jackie's lipstick from her moth, one of them whistled. She slipped inside and closed the door, feeling her lips purse into that look of mock modesty and consciousness of beauty she had seen on the faces of other women but never felt on her own.

It was only when she lifted the receiver and touched the dial that she realised. She had no money. *She had no money.* For years now she had bought her way into everything and out of everything; always about her person had been the shiny blue book and the wad of notes. But at this moment when she wanted to do something that even the poorest could afford she had no money, not even a few coppers.

It didn't matter. She could walk. Independence was like a tonic, invigorating and joyous, and it was coupled with a new dependence—on Andrew.

The lights of the car caught her in their beam as she stepped from the box. For a moment she thought it was Harry returning for her and pity fought with indignation. Dazzled, she blinked and moved into the light. This car was small, red, gay.

'Andrew,' she said as calmly as if they were meeting by a long-arranged appointment.

'Bell, darling!' He jumped out of the car and took

her in his arms. The loiterers again broke into whistles. Andrew didn't seem to notice them. 'I've been looking for you everywhere. I thought you'd run away from me. I've even been into The Boadicea to see if you were with Justin. Where have you been?'

'Seeing ghosts,' she said. I'll tell you all about it, she had been about to add. The words died and she smiled instead. Tell him about it, tell him that she had suspected her own husband of murder, of adultery, or outrageous deception? No marriage, especially so young a one as theirs, could survive it. Dependence and trust, she thought, time and patience. Time would clear up all the mysteries that remained.

Suddenly exhausted, the last spark of energy used up, she got into the car. She moved her body carefully, treasuring it and longing for the first stir of life. But when they got home he would ask her again where she had been and she would have to tell him. The answer came to her. To whom does a woman go when she suspects pregnancy but to her own doctor? Leaving Andrew without a word, running down to the High Street in the rain, all that was compatible with her hopes and fears.

For a moment she didn't speak. He was looking at her tenderly. 'I've just seen someone we used to know.' Hesitating, he chose his words with care. 'She was outside the Feasts', getting into an enormous Jaguar with a dented wing.'

'I know.'

'You've seen her too? I didn't speak to her,' he said. 'I was looking for you.'

EPILOGUE

ALICE TUCKED THE BABY UP IN HIS PRAM. HE WAS ALready asleep, a placid olive-skinned child with his father's black hair. She wheeled the pram into the shade of the diminutive porch. Andrew liked to see him there when he came home from afternoon school.

Now she had a whole two hours before her in which to read the book. It had arrived from the publisher's by the last post and for the hundredth time she read the title: *Trollope and The House of Commons* by Andrew Fielding. Some people said that artistic creation was like giving birth to a child and theirs had been a simultaneous gestation.

Her eye caught the name Saulsby in the second chapter. She smiled, shamefacedly recalling a different reaction. She had kept her resolution never to tell him what she had suspected, but some questions had to be asked.

'Why didn't you recognise the name when I asked you? You remember, I'd come back from Orphingham and you'd got my tea ready?'

He had laughed at her then, holding her tightly in his arms to take away the sting of mockery. 'What does Saulsby sound like when you say it with your mouth full of marzipan cake?'

'I see. Oh, Andrew, you thought I said *Salisbury.*'

'There must be one in every English country town.'

Still smiling, she turned the page, marvelling that a seven-letter word, once the cause of so much anguish, was now just a tiny jigsaw piece in the general pattern of contentment.

About the Author

Ruth Rendell "the best mystery writer... anywhere in the English-speaking world" (*Boston Sunday Globe*), is the author of *The New Girl Friend, An Unkindness of Ravens, The Tree of Hands, The Killing Doll, Speaker of Mandarin, The Fever Tree and Other Stories of Suspense, Master of the Moor, Death Notes, The Lake of Darkness, From Doon with Death, Sins of the Fathers, Wolf to the Slaughter, The Best Man to Die,* and many other mysteries. She now has five major awards for her work: two Edgars from the Mystery Writers of America for her short stories "The New Girl Friend" and "The Fallen Curtain"; *Current Crime*'s Silver Cup for the best British crime novel of 1975, *Shake Hands Forever*; the Crime Writer's Association's Golden Dagger for 1976's best crime novel, *A Demon in My View*; and the 1980 Arts Council National Book Award in Genre Fiction for *The Lake of Darkness*. Her books have been translated into fourteen languages. Ruth Rendell lives in Polstead, England.